JUN 1 〈 P9-ARD-609

PROPERTY OF THE

Public Library of the Town of Beverly.

PUBLIC LIBRARY OF THE TOWN OF BEVERLY.

1855.

WITHDRAWN

WITHDRAWN

THE

ASSAULT

HARRY MULISCH

THE ASSAULT

TRANSLATED FROM THE DUTCH
BY CLAIRE NICOLAS WHITE

PANTHEON BOOKS, NEW YORK

Translation copyright © 1985 by Random House Inc.
All rights reserved under International and Pan-American
Copyright Conventions.
Published in the United States by
Pantheon Books, a division of Random House, Inc., New York, and
simultaneously in Canada by Random House of Canada Limited, Toronto.
Originally published in the Netherlands as *De Aanslag* by de
Bezige Bij. Copyright © 1982 by Harry Mulisch, Amsterdam.
Library of Congress Cataloging in Publication Data
Mulisch, Harry, 1927–
The assault.
Translation of: De aanslag.
1. Netherlands—History—German occupation, 1940–1945—Fiction.
I. Title.
PT5860.M85A6313   1985   839.3'1364   84-22623
ISBN 0-394-54245-2
Manufactured in the United States of America
First American Edition
Book design by Susan Mitchell

"By then day had broken everywhere, but here it was still night—no, more than night."

Pliny the Younger
Letters, IV, 16

THE

ASSAULT

Far, far back during the Second World War, a certain Anton Steenwijk lived with his parents and his brother on the outskirts of Haarlem. There four houses stood close together along a quay that bordered the water for about a hundred meters. After a gentle curve, the quay straightened out and became an ordinary street. Each house was surrounded by a garden and had a little balcony, bay windows, and a steep roof, giving it the air of a modest villa. The rooms on the top floor all had slanted walls. The houses were somewhat dilapidated and in need of paint, for their upkeep had already been neglected during the thirties. Harking back to lighter-hearted days, each bore a brave sign with its name: Hideaway, Carefree, Home at Last, Bide-a-Wee.

Anton lived in the second house from the left, the one with the thatched roof. If it had not already been called Carefree when the family rented it shortly before the War, his father would have preferred to name it something like Eleuthera, written in Greek letters. Even before the catastrophe occurred, Anton used to think that Carefree meant a place where cares entered freely, not a place free from cares; just as someone could think priceless meant without cost, rather than beyond price.

The Beumers, an ailing retired attorney and his wife, lived in Hideaway. Anton sometimes dropped in on them for a cup of tea and cake, in the days when there were still such things as tea and cake—that is to say, long before the beginning of this story, which is the story of an accident. Sometimes Mr. Beumer read him a chapter from *The Three Musketeers*.

Mr. Korteweg was the neighbor in Home at Last, on the other side of Anton's house. Formerly a second mate in the merchant marine, he was out of work now because of the War. After the death of his wife, his daughter Karin, a nurse, had moved back home. Anton sometimes dropped in here also, through an opening in the backyard hedge. Karin was always friendly, but her father paid no attention to him.

There wasn't much socializing on that quay. The most aloof neighbors of all were the Aartses, who had lived in Bide-a-Wee since the beginning of the War. It was said that he worked for an insurance company, though no one was really sure.

Apparently these four houses had been intended as the beginning of a new development, but nothing more came of it. They were surrounded by fallow fields overgrown with weeds and bushes, and even some tall trees. It was on these undeveloped lots that Anton spent most of his time, playing with other children from a neighborhood further away. Occasionally in the late twilight when his mother forgot to call him in, a fragrant stillness would rise and fill him with expectations—of what, he didn't know. Something to do with later, when he'd be grown up—things that would happen then. Something to do with the motionless earth, the leaves, two sparrows that suddenly twittered and scratched about. Life someday would be like those evenings, mysterious and endless, when he had been forgotten.

The cobblestones on the road in front of the house were laid in a herringbone pattern. The street did not have a sidewalk. It petered out into a grassy bank that sloped gently down to the towpath, where it was pleasant to lie on one's back. The wide canal's uneven, winding bank showed that it had been a river at one time. Across the water stood a few farmhands' cottages and small farms; to the right, where the bank curved, was a windmill that never turned. Behind the farms, the meadows stretched out to the horizon. Still further lay Amsterdam. Before the War, his father had told him, one could see the glow of city lights reflected against the clouds. Anton had been there a few times, to the zoo and the Rijksmuseum, and to his uncle's to spend the night.

Lying on the grassy bank and staring into the distance, he sometimes had to pull in his legs because a man who seemed to step out of another century came walking along the trampled towpath. The man had one end of a pole several yards long attached to his waist, while the other end was fastened to the prow of a barge. Walking with heavy steps, he pushed against the pole and thus moved the boat through the water. Usually a woman wearing an apron, her hair in a knot, stood at the wheel, and a child played on deck.

At other times the man remained on deck and walked forward along the side of the barge, dragging the pole behind him through the water. When he reached the bow, he planted the stick sideways in the bottom of the canal, grasped it firmly, and walked backwards, so that he pushed the boat forward beneath his feet. This specially pleased Anton: a man walking backwards to push something forward, while staying in the same place himself. There was something very strange about it, but it was his secret that he didn't mention to anyone. Not till later, when he described it to his children, did he realize what primitive times he had witnessed. Only in movies about Africa and Asia could one still see such things.

Several times a day sailing barges, heavily laden ships with dark-brown sails, appeared silently around the first bend and, driven onward by the invisible wind, disappeared around the next.

The motorboats were different. Pitching, their prows would tear the water into a V shape that spread until it reached both sides of the canal. There the water would begin to lap up and down, even though the boat was already far away. Then the waves bounced back and formed an inverted V, which interfered with the original V, reached the opposite shore transformed, and bounced back again—until all across the water a complicated braiding of ripples developed which went on changing for several minutes, then finally smoothed out.

Each time, Anton tried to figure out exactly how this happened, but each time the pattern became so complex that he could no longer follow it.

FIRST EPISODE

1945

1

It was about half past seven in the evening. The coal stove had been purring softly, fed by a few bits of wood, and then gone out again. Anton was sitting at the table in the back room with his parents and Peter. A zinc cylinder about the size of a flowerpot was standing on a dish. A thin pipe stuck out on top, split in two like a Y, and from little holes at its tips emerged two pointed, blinding-white flames that were aimed at each other. This gadget cast a dull light through the room. Silhouetted against the deep shadows, the much-darned and -mended laundry was hung up to dry. The light also revealed mounds of unironed shirts, a box to keep the food warm, and two piles of books from his father's study: the row on the dresser to be read, the stack of novels on the floor to light the emergency stove on which the cooking was done, whenever there was anything to cook. Newspapers had not appeared in months.

Except for sleeping, all daily life took place here, in what used to be the dining room. The sliding doors were kept closed. Behind them, on the street side, the living room had not been used all winter. Even in daytime its curtains remained closed against the cold, so that the house looked uninhabited from the quay side.

It was January, nineteen forty-five. Almost all of Europe had been liberated and was once more rejoicing, drinking, making love, and beginning to forget the War. But every day Haarlem looked more like one of those spent gray clinkers that they used to take out of the stove, when there had still been coal to burn.

A dark-blue sweater lay on the table in front of his mother. She had already unraveled half of it. In her left hand she held the growing ball of wool around which her right hand quickly wound the sweater's yarn. Anton watched the yarn speeding back and forth while the sweater vanished from the world. The sleeves, spread out flat, looked as if they were holding on, resisting this transformation into a ball with all their might. His mother gave him a fleeting smile, and he lowered his eyes to his book.

His mother's blond tresses were coiled over her ears like two ammonite shells. Now and then she stopped and took a sip of her cold tea substitute, made with melted snow from the backyard because the pipes were frozen. She had a cavity in her tooth that couldn't be treated just then; to relieve the pain she had found a leftover clove in the kitchen to put on the sore spot, just as her grandmother used to do. She sat up straight, but her husband across the table was bent over, reading a book. His dark hair, turning gray, grew in a semicircle like a horseshoe around his bald pate. From time to time he blew into his hands, which were large and clumsy, though he was not a laborer but a clerk at the district court.

Anton wore his brother's hand-me-downs, while Peter was dressed in an oversized black suit of his father's. Peter was seventeen, and since he had begun to grow fast just when there was less and less to eat, his body looked as if it had been put together with sticks of kindling. He was doing his homework. He had not set foot in the street for two months, because he was old enough to be rounded up by the police and sent to a labor camp in Germany. He was still only in his second year of high school, for he had failed twice. Now he was being taught by his father, homework and all, so he wouldn't fall behind even more.

The brothers didn't look anything alike; neither did their parents. Some couples have a striking resemblance to one another (possibly this means that the wife looks like her husband's mother, and the husband like his wife's father, or something even more complicated, which no doubt it is). The Steenwijk couple, however, were two distinct entities. Of the sons, Peter had the blond-and-blue coloring of his mother, Anton his father's dark-brown complexion, even to the way their nut-brown skin grew darker around the eyes.

Anton wasn't going to school just then either. He was in the sixth grade, but because of the coal shortage, the Christmas vacation had been extended until the end of the freezing weather.

He was hungry, but he knew that he wouldn't get his sticky gray sandwich spread with sugar beet syrup until morning. That afternoon he had stood in line for an hour at the central kitchen in the nursery school. The pushcart, its pans guarded by a policeman with a rifle on his back, had not entered the street till after dark. Once Anton's tickets had been punched, four ladles of watery soup were dished up into the pot he had brought along. On his way home across the lots he had tasted just a little of the warm, sour concoction. Luckily he would be going to bed soon; in his dreams there was always peace.

No one spoke. Outside too, all was quiet. The War had lasted forever and would last forever. No radio, no telephone, nothing. The flames hissed. Now and then they sputtered softly. Wrapped in a scarf, his feet stuck into a foot warmer that his mother had made out of an old shopping bag, Anton was reading an article in *Nature and Mechanics*. For his birthday he had been given a secondhand bound copy of the 1938 edition: "A Letter to Posterity." A photograph showed a group of well-fed Americans in their shirt sleeves looking up at a large, shiny capsule shaped like a torpedo that hung vertically above their heads. The capsule was about to be lowered into a hole fifteen meters deep. In five thousand years it was to be dug up and opened by posterity, which would then learn what human civilization had been like at the time of the World's Fair in New York. Inside the capsule, made of amazingly durable "cupalloy," was a fire-resistant glass cylinder filled with hundreds of objects: a microfilm containing a survey of science, technology, and the arts in ten million words and a thousand illustrations, newspapers, catalogs, famous novels, the Bible, of course, and the Our Father in three hundred languages. Also messages from famous men, movies of the terrible Japanese bombings of Canton in 1937, seeds, an electric plug, a slide rule, and all kinds of other things—even a lady's hat that was in fashion during the autumn of 1938. All the important libraries and museums in the world had received a document specifying the location of the cement-covered capsule, so that it could be retrieved in the seventieth century. But why, Anton wondered, would they have to wait until precisely the year 6938? Wouldn't it be of interest long before then?

"Papa, how long is five thousand years ago?"

"Precisely five thousand years," said Steenwijk without looking up from his book.

"Yes, I know that. But was there already . . . I mean . . ."

"Say what you mean."

"Well, did people, just like now, have . . ."

"Civilization?" asked his mother.

"Yes."

"Why don't you let the boy formulate it himself?" asked Steenwijk, looking at her over the top of his glasses. And then to Anton, "Civilization was still in its infancy, in Egypt and in Mesopotamia. Why do you ask?"

"Because here it says that more than . . ."

"Ready!" said Peter and looked up from his dictionaries and grammar. He pushed his homework over to his father and came to stand beside Anton.

"What are you reading?"

"Nothing," said Anton, bending over the book, hiding it from his brother with his chest and crossed arms.

"Stop that, Tonny," said his mother and pulled him upright.

"I'm never allowed to look at his!"

"That's a dirty lie, Anton Mussert," said Peter, upon which Anton held his nose and began to sing in a nasal voice:

> For I was born with bad luck
> And I'll die with bad luck . . .

"Quiet!" Steenwijk called out and slapped the table with the flat of his hand.

That his name should be Anton, like the leader of the Dutch Nazi Party, was a nuisance of course, and the cause of much teasing. During the war, Fascists often called their sons Anton or Adolf, sometimes even Anton Adolf, and proudly sent out birth announcements decorated with Germanic runes, or with the emblem of the Dutch Nazi Party, a wolf trap. Later, whenever he met someone with either of those names, or with the nicknames Ton or Dolf, he'd try and find out if they had been born during the War. If so, it was a sure sign that their parents had been collaborators, and not just by half. The name Anton became acceptable again ten or fifteen years after the War, which goes to show how insignificant Anton Mussert actually was. For of course the name Adolf still won't do. Not until people are called Adolf again will the Second World War be really behind us. But that means we'd have to have a third world war, so we'd better do without Adolfs altogether.

As for the jingle that Anton had been singing in self-defense, it too has become meaningless. It was a nasal refrain sung by a radio comedian called Peter Pech, at a time when radios were still allowed. In Dutch, Pech means bad luck. But there are many more things about those times that have become meaningless today, especially to Anton himself.

"Why don't you come and sit next to me?" said Steenwijk to Peter, taking up the homework. In a solemn voice he began reading the translation aloud:

Just as when rivers, swollen with rain and melting snow, streaming down from the mountains to a valley basin and welling up out of abundant springs, gather in their hollow beds—and far away in the mountain the shepherd hears their muffled roar—so sounded the shouting and the painful struggle of the soldiers engaged in a hand-to-hand battle.

"How beautiful this is," said Steenjwijk, leaning back and taking off his glasses.

"Sure, great," said Peter. "Specially after I've been working on it an hour and a half, that lousy sentence."

"It's worth a day's work. Look at the way he evokes nature, but only obliquely, in comparison. Did you notice? What one remembers are not the fighting soldiers, but the image of nature—and that goes on existing. The battle has vanished, but the rivers are still there, one can still hear them, and then one becomes, oneself, that shepherd. It's as if he wanted to say that all of existence is a metaphor for another reality, and that the whole point is to grasp that other reality."

"Then that other reality must be the War," said Peter.

Steenwijk pretended not to have heard.

"Very well translated, my boy. Except for *one* mistake. They are not rivers, plural, that come together, but two rivers."

"Where does it say that?"

"Here: *symballeton*, that's a duality, the coming together of two things, two. Now the two armies also make sense. This is a form you find only in Homer. Remember the word 'symbol,' which comes from *symballo*, 'to bring together,' 'meeting.' Do you know what a *symbolon* was?"

"No," said Peter in a tone implying that he couldn't care less.

"What was it, Papa?" asked Anton.

"It was a stone that they broke in two. Say I am a guest

in another city, and I ask my host whether he would be willing to receive you too. How can he be sure that you really are my son? We make a *symbolon*. He keeps one half, and at home I give you the other. So then when you get there, they fit together exactly."

"That's great," said Anton. "I'm going to try that someday."

Groaning, Peter turned away. "Why in God's name should I learn all that?"

"Not in God's name," said Steenwijk, peering at him over his glasses. "In the name of *humanitas*. You'll see how much pleasure it will give you for the rest of your life."

Peter slammed his books shut, piled them up, and said in a strange tone of voice: "Who looks at man, laughs if he can."

"Now what has that got to do with anything, Peter?" asked his mother. With her tongue she pushed the clove back in place.

"Nothing."

"I'm afraid so," said Steenwijk. "*Sunt pueri pueri pueri puerilia tractant.*"

The sweater had disappeared, and Mrs. Steenwijk stowed the ball of yarn in her sewing basket.

"Come, let's play a game before we go to bed."

"To bed already?" said Peter.

"We've got to save gas. We only have enough for a few days."

Mrs. Steenwijk pulled the box out of the drawer of the dresser, pushed the lamp aside, and unfolded the game board.

"I want green," said Anton.

Peter looked at him and tapped his forehead.

"Do you really think green will make you win?"

"Sure."

"We'll see about that."

Steenwijk laid down his book. A moment later the only

15

sounds were those of the dice being shaken and the pawns being moved across the board. It was almost eight o'clock: curfew. Outside all was as still as it must be on the moon.

2

In the silence that was Holland then, six shots suddenly rang out. First, one echoed through the street, then two more in rapid succession, and a few seconds later, a fourth and a fifth. After a moment came a kind of scream, followed by a sixth shot. Anton, about to throw the dice, froze and looked at his mother, his mother at his father, his father at the sliding doors; but Peter picked up the cover of the carbon lamp and put it over the flame.

Suddenly, all was dark. Peter stood up, stumbled forward, opened the sliding doors, and peered through a crack in the curtains of the bay window. Freezing-cold air immediately streamed in from the parlor.

"They shot someone!" he said. "Someone's lying there." He hurried into the front hall.

"Peter!" cried his mother.

Anton heard her follow. He jumped up himself and ran to the bay window. Unerringly he dodged all the invisible furniture that he hadn't seen for months: the armchairs, the low, round table with the lace doily under the glass plate, the dresser with the ceramic platter and the portraits of his grandparents. The curtains, the windowsill, everything was icy cold. No one had breathed in this room for so long that there weren't even any frost flowers on the windowpanes. It was a moonless night, but the frozen snow held the light of the stars. At first he thought that Peter had been talking nonsense, but now he too saw it through the left side of the bay window.

In the middle of the deserted street, in front of Mr. Korteweg's house, lay a bicycle with its upended front wheel still turning—a dramatic effect later much used in close-ups in every movie about the Resistance. Limping, Peter ran along the garden path into the street. The last few weeks he'd had a boil on his toe that would not heal, and his mother had cut a piece out of his shoe to ease the pain. He knelt beside a man lying motionless in the gutter not far from the bicycle. The man's right hand was resting on the edge of the sidewalk, as if he had made himself comfortable. Anton saw the shimmer of black boots and the iron plates on the heels.

In a whisper that was surprisingly loud, his mother called Peter from the doorstep to come in at once. He stood up, looked to right and left along the quay and then back at the man, and limped home.

"It's Ploeg!" Anton heard him say a minute later in the hall, a tone of triumph in his voice. "Dead as a doornail, if you ask me."

Anton too knew Fake Ploeg, Chief Inspector of Police, the greatest murderer and traitor in Haarlem. He passed by regularly on his way between his office and his house in Heemstede. A big, square-shouldered man with a rough face, he was usually dressed in a hat, a brown sports jacket, and a shirt with a tie. But he wore black riding pants and high boots, and he radiated violence, hate, and fear. His son, also named Fake, was in Anton's class. From the bay window Anton stared at the boots. He knew those, all right, because Fake had been brought to school a couple of times by his father on the back of that very bicycle. Each time they arrived at the school entrance, everyone fell silent. The father looked about with a mocking glance, but after he left, the son went in with downcast eyes and had to manage as best he could.

"Tonny!" His mother called. "Get away from that window!"

On the second day of school when nobody knew who he was yet, Fake had appeared in the pale-blue uniform and black-and-orange cap of the Nazi youth organization. That was in September, shortly after Mad Tuesday, when everyone thought the liberators were on their way and most National Socialists and collaborators had fled to the German border or beyond. Fake sat all alone at his desk in the classroom and pulled out his books. Mr. Bos, the science teacher, stood in the doorway, his arm against the doorjamb to keep out the other students; he had called back those who had already entered. He announced to Fake that there would be no teaching students in uniform, it hadn't gotten that far and would never get that far, and he should go home and change. Fake said nothing, did not look back at the doorway but remained motionless. After a while the principal edged through the students and began to whisper excitedly to the teacher, who wouldn't give in.

Anton stood in the front of the crowd and, under Bos's arm, stared at the back of the boy in the empty room. Then, slowly, Fake turned around and looked him straight in the eyes. All at once Anton was overcome by a strange pity for him. How could Fake possibly go home, with that father of his? Before he knew what he was doing, Anton dove under Mr. Bos's arm and sat down at his desk. This broke down the general resistance of the others. After school the principal stood waiting for him in the hall, caught him briefly by the arm, and whispered that he had probably saved Mr. Bos's life. Anton didn't quite know what to do with this compliment. He never told anyone at home about it, and the incident was never mentioned again.

The body in the gutter. The wheel had stopped turning. Above, the amazing starry sky. His eyes were used to the darkness now, and he could see ten times better than before. Orion lifting his sword, the Milky Way, one brilliant, shiny planet, probably Jupiter—not in centuries had Holland's skies been this clear. On the horizon two slowly moving searchlights crossed each other and fanned out, but no plane could be heard. He noticed that he was still holding one of the dice in his hand and put it in his pocket.

As he was about to move away from the window, he saw Mr. Korteweg come out of his house, followed by Karin. Korteweg picked Ploeg up by the shoulders, Karin by the boots, and together they began dragging him through the snow, Karin walking backwards.

"Look at that," said Anton.

His mother and Peter were just in time to see them deposit the body in front of Carefree. Karin threw Ploeg's cap, which had fallen off, onto his body. Her father moved the bicycle to the road in front of Carefree. The next moment they had disappeared into Home at Last.

Everyone was speechless in the bay window at the Steenwijks'. The quay was once more deserted, everything was as quiet as it had been, yet everything had changed. The dead man now lay with his arms above his head, the right hand clasping a gun, the long coat gathered at the waist, as if Ploeg had fallen from a great height. Now Anton clearly recognized the large face, its hair slicked down and brushed back, practically undisturbed.

"God dammit!" screamed Peter suddenly, his voice breaking.

"Hey, hey, watch it," came Steenwijk's voice from the darkness of the back room. He was still sitting at the table.

"They put him down in front of our house, the bastards!" Peter cried. "Jesus Christ! We've got to get him out of here before the Krauts come."

"Don't get involved," said Mrs. Steenwijk. "We had nothing to do with it."

"No, except that now he's lying in front of our door! Why do you suppose they did that? Because the Krauts are going to retaliate, of course. Just like before, at the Leidse Canal."

"We didn't do anything wrong, Peter."

"As if they care! You're dealing with Krauts." He left the room. "Come on Anton, hurry; you and I can do it."

"Are you crazy?" Mrs. Steenwijk cried. She choked, cleared her throat, and spat out the clove. "What do you want to do?"

"Put him back—or at Mrs. Beumer's."

"At Mrs. Beumer's? How can you think of such a thing?"

"Why not at Mrs. Beumer's? Mrs. Beumer had nothing to do with it either! If only the river weren't frozen . . . We'll see what we can do."

"No you don't!"

Mrs. Steenwijk rushed out of the room. In the dim light that fell through the transom into the front hall, Anton saw that his mother had posted herself in front of the door; Peter was trying to push her aside. He heard her turn the key as she called, "Willem, why don't you say something?"

"Yes . . . yes . . ." Anton heard his father's voice, still in the back room. "I . . ."

In the distance, shots rang out again.

"If he'd been hit a few seconds later, he'd be lying at Mrs. Beumer's now," called Peter.

"Yes . . ." said Steenwijk softly, his voice breaking in an odd way, "But that is not the case."

"Not the case! It wasn't the case that he was lying here, either, but now it *is* the case!" Peter said suddenly, "In fact, I'm going to take him back. I'll just do it alone."

He turned to run toward the kitchen door, but with a cry of pain tripped over the pile of logs and branches from the last trees his mother had chopped down in the empty lots.

"Peter, for God's sake!" cried Mrs. Steenwijk. "You're playing with your life!"

"That's exactly what *you're* doing, dammit."

Before Peter could pick himself up, Anton turned the key in the kitchen door and threw it into the hall, where it clattered and became invisible; then he ran to the front door and did the same with the house key.

"God dammit," cried Peter, almost in tears. "You're pathetic, pathetic, all of you."

He went to the back room, tore aside the curtains, and with his good foot pushed against the french doors. They burst open with a crash, sending strips of paper insulation flying, and suddenly Anton saw his father's silhouette outlined against the snow. He was still sitting at the table.

As Peter disappeared into the garden, Anton ran back to the bay window. He saw his brother appear around the house, climb over the fence, and grip Ploeg by the boots. At that moment he seemed to hesitate, perhaps because of all the blood, perhaps because he couldn't decide which direction to take. But before he could do anything, shouts echoed at the end of the quay.

"Halt! Stand still! Hands up!"

Three men approached, bicycling hard. They threw their bikes down on the street and began running. Peter dropped Ploeg's legs, pulled the gun out of Ploeg's hand, ran without limping to the Kortewegs' fence, and disappeared behind their house. The men screamed at each other. One of them, wearing a cap and an overcoat, took a shot at Peter and chased after him.

Anton felt his mother's warmth beside him.

"What was that? Are they shooting at Peter? Where is he?"

"Out in back."

With wide eyes Anton watched everything. The second man, who wore a Military Police uniform, ran back to his bicycle, jumped on, and rode away at full speed. The third, who was in civilian clothes, slid down the other side of the embankment and crouched on the towpath, holding a gun with both hands.

Anton dove below the windowsill and turned around. His

mother had disappeared. At the table the silhouette of his
father was a little more bent than before, as if he were pray-
ing. Then Anton heard his mother, in the backyard, whisper
Peter's name into the night. It was as if the cold which now
streamed into the house emanated from her back. There
was no further sound. Anton saw and heard everything, but
somehow he was no longer quite there. One part of him was
already somewhere else, or nowhere at all. He was under-
nourished, and stiff now with cold, but that wasn't all. This
moment—his father cut out in black against the snow, his
mother outside on the terrace under the starlight—became
eternal, detached itself from all that had come before and
all that would follow. It became part of him and began its
journey through the rest of his life, until finally it would
explode like a soap bubble, after which it might as well
never have happened.

His mother came in.

"Tonny? Where are you? Do you see him?"

"No."

"What should we do? Perhaps he's hiding somewhere."
Agitated, she walked outside again and then came back.
Suddenly she went to her husband and pulled at his shoul-
ders.

"Will you ever wake up? They're shooting at Peter! Perhaps he's been hit already."

Slowly Steenwijk stood up. Without a word, tall and thin,
he left the room. A moment later he returned wearing a
scarf and his black bowler hat. As he was about to enter the
garden from the terrace, he drew back. Anton could hear
that he was trying to call Peter's name, but only a hoarse
sound came out. Defeated, he turned back. He came in and
went to sit, trembling, on the chair next to the stove. After a
few moments he said, "Please forgive me, Thea . . . forgive
me . . ." Mrs. Steenwijk's hands wrestled with each other.

"Everything has gone so well until now, and now, at the

end . . . Anton, put on your coat. Oh God, where can that boy be?"

"Perhaps he went into the Kortewegs'," said Anton. "He took Ploeg's gun."

From the silence which followed his words he understood that this was something terrible.

"Did you really see that?"

"Just as those men came . . . Like this . . . as he ran away . . ."

In the soft, powdery light which now hung about the rooms, he acted out a short sprint and, leaning over, pulled an imaginary pistol out of an imaginary hand.

"You don't suppose he . . ." Mrs. Steenwijk caught her breath. "I'm going to Korteweg's right now."

She started to run into the garden, but Anton followed and said, "Watch out! There's another man out there somewhere."

As her husband had done before her, she drew back from the freezing silence. Nothing stirred. There was the garden, and beyond it the barren, snow-covered lots. Anton too stood motionless. Everything was still—and yet time went by. It was as if everything grew radiant with the passage of time, like pebbles at the bottom of a brook. Peter had disappeared, a corpse lay in front of the door, and all about them the armed men remained motionless. Anton had the feeling that by doing something which was within his power but which he could not quite think of, he could undo everything and return to the way they had been before, sitting around the table playing a game. It was as if he had forgotten a name remembered a hundred times before and now on the tip of his tongue, but the harder he tried to recall it, the more elusive it became. Or it was like the time when he had suddenly realized that he was breathing in and out continuously and must make sure to keep doing it or else suffocate—and at that moment he almost did suffocate.

Motorcycles sounded in the distance; also, he heard the noise of a car.

"Come in, Mama," said Anton.

"Yes . . . I'll close the doors."

He could tell from her voice that she stood on the edge of something she could not master. It seemed as if he was the only one who kept his wits, and that, of course, was as it should be, for a future aviator. In the Air Force difficult situations might also arise: at the eye of a cyclone, for instance, the wind is calm and the sun shines, but the pilot must fly out into the turmoil of weather, or else he'll get lost and run out of fuel.

Now the motorcycles and the car could be heard out front on the quay, while more cars—heavier ones—seemed to be approaching in the distance. So far, everything was still all right; nothing had changed, really—except of course that Peter had disappeared. How could anything really change?

Then there it was. Squeaking tires, shouting in German, the iron clatter of boots jumping onto the street. Now and then a bright light flashed through the split between the curtains. Anton tiptoed to the bay window. Everywhere soldiers with rifles and machine guns, motorcycles coming and going, trucks with still more soldiers; a military ambulance out of which a stretcher was being pulled. Suddenly he yanked the curtains closed and turned around.

"Here they are," he said into the darkness. At that moment there was a banging on the door, so unnecessarily loud, with the butt of a rifle, that he knew something terrible was about to happen.

"*Aufmachen*! Open at once!"

Involuntarily he fled to the back room. His mother went into the hall and called out with a trembling voice that the key was lost. But already the door was being broken down and slammed against the wall. Anton heard the mirror shatter, the one with the two carved elephants over the little side table with the twisted legs. Suddenly the hall and rooms were filled with armed men in helmets, wrapped in ice-cold air, all much too large for his mother and father's house. Already it was no longer theirs. Blinded by a lantern, Anton lifted one arm to his eyes. From beneath it he could see the shiny badge of the Field Police, and hanging from a belt, the elongated container of a gas mask, and boots caked with snow. A man in civilian dress entered the room. He wore a long black leather coat down to his ankles and on his head a hat with a lowered brim.

"*Papiere*, papers, *vorzeigen*!" he shouted. "*Schnell*, quick, all your papers, everything."

Steenwijk stood up and opened a drawer in the dresser, while his wife said: "We had nothing to do with all this."

"*Schweigen Sie*, silence!" snapped the man. He stood by the table and with the nail of his index finger flipped shut the book that Steenwijk had been reading. "*Ethica*," he read on the cover, "*Ordine Geometrico Demonstrata. Benedictus de Spinoza*. Ach so!" He looked up. "That's what you people read here; Jew books." And then to Mrs. Steenwijk, "Just take a few steps up and down."

"What should I do?"

"Walk back and forth! Do you have shit in your ears?"

Anton saw his mother trembling all over as she paced up and down with the puzzled expression of a child. The man aimed the flashlight at her legs.

"*Das genugt*, enough," he said after a while. Not till much later when he was in college did Anton learn that the man thought he could tell by her walk whether she was Jewish.

Steenwijk stood with the papers in his hand. "*Ich* . . ."

"You might take off your hat when you talk to me."

Steenwijk took off his bowler hat and repeated, "I . . ."

"Keep your mouth shut, you pig Jew-lover." The man studied the identity papers and ration cards, then looked about him.

"Where is the fourth?"

Mrs. Steenwijk tried to say something, but it was her husband who spoke.

"My oldest son," he began with a trembling voice, "confused by this dreadful accident, has rushed out of the parental home without taking his leave, and he went in that direction." With his hat he pointed in the direction of Hideaway, where the Beumers lived.

"So," said the German, shoving the papers into his pocket. "He rushed out, did he?"

"Yes indeed."

The man made a gesture with the head. "*Abführen*. Take them away."

Then everything went at a terrible clip. They were pushed out of the house without being allowed to take anything with them, not even a coat. Vehicles stood all over the street, gray civilian cars and army trucks all mixed together, everywhere uniforms and shouting and the dancing beams of flashlights. There were soldiers leading dogs on leashes. The ambulance had gone; only Ploeg's bicycle still lay there, and a large red stain on the snow. Again Anton heard shots from somewhere. He felt his mother's hand reach for his. As he looked up he saw her face change into that of a statue, with a wide-eyed expression of horror. His father, who had once more put on his hat, kept his eyes on the ground, the way he always did when he walked. But Anton himself was filled with an ambiguous pleasure at all this busyness, all this activity after the deadly stillness of the last few months. Perhaps he was also partially hypnotized by the bright flashes of light that lit up his face again and again; but finally, finally something was happening.

Lost in his dream, he felt the grasp of his mother's hand suddenly tightening before they were torn apart.

"Tonny!"

She had already vanished somewhere behind the trucks; so had his father. A soldier dragged Anton by the arm to a van that was parked across the street, halfway up on the embankment. He made Anton get in and slammed the door behind him.

For the first time in his life he was sitting in a car. Vaguely he made out the steering wheel and the control panels. In an airplane there would be many more panels. In a Lockheed Electra, for instance, there were at least fifteen, and two steering wheels. He looked out. Nowhere did he see his parents. Where could Peter be hiding? Soldiers with flashlights were walking in and out over at Korteweg's too, but as far as he could tell, without Peter. No doubt he had managed to escape across the vacant lots. Did they know that Ploeg had first been lying in front of the Kortewegs'? There was no one in the Beumers' garden. The car windows were fogging up and he could see less and less of the street. He wiped them off, but the outlines remained blurred and distorted.

Suddenly the doors to the balcony in his parents' room were thrown open. A moment later the curtains of the living room downstairs were pushed back and all the windows smashed with rifle butts from the inside. Dazed, he looked at the rain of shattering splinters. What bastards! Where would his parents get new panes? Surely no more glass could be found. Luckily they seemed to have caused enough damage, for one by one the soldiers came outside. They left the front door open.

Nothing more happened, but they didn't leave. Some of them lit cigarettes and chatted together, hands in their pockets, stamping their feet against the cold. Others aimed their flashlights at the house, as if they enjoyed the spectacle of what they had destroyed.

Anton tried again to see his parents, but further away in the darkness, people were only shadows in the flashlights darting back and forth. Dogs were barking. His thoughts returned to before, in the room, how the man with the hat had yelled at his father . . . It was much more painful now than while it was happening. His father, who had had to take his hat off . . . he pushed the image away, wanted never to remember it again; it should never have been allowed to happen. Never in his life would he wear a bowler; after the War no one would ever be allowed to wear a hat.

He looked out and wondered. It was growing quieter. Everyone stepped back to a safe distance; no one moved. An order was given, after which a soldier walked toward the house, threw something into the middle bay window, and came running back, bent in two. There was a resounding explosion. Briefly a blinding bouquet of fire lit up the drawing room. Anton ducked. When he looked again, a second grenade exploded in the bedroom. Right after this a soldier appeared with what looked like a fire hose in his hands and a cylinder on his back. He stepped forward and began to spray the windows with long, thundering streaks of fire.

Anton couldn't believe it. Was it believable, this thing happening there? Desperately he searched for his father and mother, but because of those bright lights he couldn't see anything. One stream of smoking light after another flew into the front room, the vestibule, the bedroom, and finally onto the thatched roof. They were really doing it; this could no longer be stopped. The house was burning inside and out. All his possessions, his books by Karl May, his *Nature Studies of the Open Field*, his collection of airplane pictures, his father's library whose shelves were lined with green baize, his mother's clothes, the ball of yarn, the chairs and tables: nothing was spared.

The soldier screwed his flamethrower shut and disappeared into the darkness. Laughing and talking, a few men of the *Grüne Polizei* with carbines slung over their shoulders came forward, tucked their gloves into their belts, held up their hands to the crackling flames as if they wanted to push them back.

A little further on, another truck stopped. Standing in its open bed was a group of shivering men in civilian jackets, guarded by soldiers with machine guns. In the light of the flames he recognized them by their black helmets as SS troops. Shouts, commands. Two by two, handcuffed, the prisoners jumped down to the street and disappeared in the night. The house, dried out during the frost, was burning as greedily as an old newspaper. Anton himself began to feel the glow inside the car. The pointed flames danced through the overhanging dormer window on the left: so now his room went, but at least he felt a little warmer. Suddenly the flames broke through the roof and lit up the whole quay with a brilliant light, as in a scene at the theater.

He imagined that further on, between the cars, he caught a glimpse of his mother, her hair hanging loose, and a man running toward her. Something was taking place over there; but hardly anything could touch him anymore. He was thinking: how can they do this in the blackout? Before you know it, the English will see this and then they'll come; if only they would come . . . On the sign attached at an angle to the frame over the bay window, the name of the house, although singed, was still readable: *Carefree*. In the rooms where it had been cold for so long, hellfire now reigned. Everywhere black soot fluttered down onto the snow.

A few minutes later, something began to creak inside and the house collapsed under a fountain of sparks as high as a tower. The dogs barked; the soldiers who had been warming themselves jumped back, one of them tripping over Ploeg's bicycle and landing full length on the street. The others doubled up with laughter, and at the same time a machine gun began to rattle at the end of the quay. Anton lay on his side and curled up, his wrists crossed under his chin.

When the German with the long coat opened the door and saw him lying there, he caught his breath.

"*Scheisse*," he said. "Shit."

Anton had to creep into the narrow space behind the seats

where he could hardly see a thing. The man in the long coat sat down next to the army driver and lit a cigarette. The motor began to sputter, the driver wiped the fog off the front window, and for the first time Anton rode in a car. The houses were all dark; there was not a soul to be seen in the streets except now and then small groups of Germans. The two men did not talk. They drove to Heemstede and after a few minutes stopped in front of the police station, which was guarded by two cops.

The warm waiting room was filled with men, most of them in German or Dutch uniforms. Anton's mouth immediately began to water at the smell of fried eggs, yet he saw no one eat. There were electric lights, and all the men were smoking cigarettes. He was made to sit down on a chair near the tall pot-bellied stove, where the heat embraced him. The German spoke with a Dutch Inspector of Police, occasionally motioning with his chin in Anton's direction. For the first time Anton saw the man clearly. But what he saw then, in 1945, was different from what he would see now. The German was about forty years old and actually had that lean, hardened face with the horizontal scar beneath the left cheekbone—a type no longer used except by directors of comedies or grade B movies. Today only babyish Himmler faces are still artistically acceptable; but then it was not an artistic matter, then he really did look like a fanatical Nazi, and it wasn't funny. A little later he left without glancing back at Anton.

A police sergeant carrying a gray horse blanket over his arm came over and told Anton to follow him. In the hall a second policeman joined them. He carried a bunch of keys in his hand.

"What do we have now?" he said when he saw Anton. "Are we locking up children too? Or is he a little Jew?"

"Don't ask so many questions," said the sergeant. At the end of the hall they followed each other down the cellar stairs. Anton turned back to the sergeant and asked:

"Are my father and mother coming too?" The sergeant did not look at him.

"I know nothing. We had nothing to do with this incident."

Downstairs it was cold again. A short hall led, below all sorts of pipes and wires, to some iron doors painted with yellowish paint full of rust spots. A weak, bare light bulb burned on the ceiling.

"Where do we have room?" asked the sergeant.

"Nowhere. He'll have to sleep on the floor."

The sergeant's eyes swept around the hall, as if he could see what was behind each door.

"How about there?" he said, and pointed to the farthest door on the left.

"But that's the Social Democrat—in solitary."

"Do what I say."

The policeman unbolted the door, and the sergeant threw the horse blanket onto a cot standing against the wall.

"It's just for tonight," he said to Anton. "Try to get some sleep." Then, in the direction of the corner Anton could not see, "You'll have company, but keep the boy out of it, will you? He's had enough misery, thanks to you."

Anton felt a hand pushing him in the back and crossed over the doorstep into the dark cell. The door closed behind him, and he saw nothing more.

Groping, he reached for the cot. All about him he could feel the presence of the man who must be in there somewhere. He folded his hands in his lap and listened to the voices in the hall. A bit later he heard boots walking up the stairs, and all grew quiet. Now he heard the other one breathing.

"Why are you here?"

The gentle voice of a woman. Suddenly it was as if a great

danger had been averted. He opened his eyes wide to see, but the darkness filled them like black water. Now in the other cells he could hear muffled voices.

"They set our house on fire."

As he said it, he could hardly believe himself that there should be nothing left but a smouldering ruin between Hideaway and Home at Last. It took a while before she answered.

"Why did they? Did it happen just now?"

"Yes ma'am."

"Why?"

"In revenge. A fellow had been shot, but we had nothing to do with it. We weren't allowed to take anything along."

"Oh shit," she said. Then, after a while, "Jesus. Were you maybe at home alone?"

"No, with my father and mother and my brother." He noticed that his eyes were closing all by themselves. He opened them wide, but it made little difference.

"Where are they now?"

"I don't know."

"Did the Germans take them away?"

"Yes. At least, my father and mother."

"And your brother?"

"He escaped. He wanted . . ." It was the first time that he had to cry just a little. "Now look at me . . ." He was ashamed but couldn't help it.

"Come and sit next to me."

He stood up and felt his way step by step in her direction.

"Yes, here I am," she said. "Put out your hand." He touched her fingers; she took hold of his hand and pulled him close. On the cot she embraced him with one arm and with her other hand pressed his head against her breast. She smelled of sweat but also of something else, something sweetish that he couldn't identify. Perhaps it was perfume. Within the darkness there was a second darkness in which he heard her heart pound, really much too hard for someone who was just comforting someone else.

As he calmed down, he began to see a pale strip of light under the door and kept his eyes focused on it. She must have caught a glimpse of him when he entered. She draped her blanket around the two of them and held him firmly against her. She was not as warm as the stove upstairs, yet at the same time she was so much warmer. Once more tears welled in his eyes, but now in a different way. He would have liked to ask her why she was in prison, but didn't dare. Perhaps she had been dealing on the black market. He heard her swallow.

"I don't know your name," she whispered. "And I shouldn't know it. You can't know mine either, but will you never forget one thing for the rest of your life?"

"What's that?"

"How old are you?"

"Almost thirteen, ma'am."

"Oh, stop calling me ma'am. Listen. They'll try and make you believe all kinds of things, but you must never forget that it was the Krauts who burned down your house. Whoever did it, did it, and not anyone else."

"Of course I know that," said Anton, a little offended. "I saw it with my own eyes, after all."

"Yes, but they did it because that pig had been liquidated, and they'll blame the Underground and say they were forced to do it. They'll tell you that the Underground knew what would happen and therefore the Underground is responsible."

"Oh," said Anton drawing himself up a little and trying to formulate what he thought about it. "But if that's the case, then . . . then no one's ever at fault. Then everyone can just do as they please."

"Do you happen to know, by the way . . ." she began hesitantly, "what that fellow's name was?"

"Ploeg," he said. Quickly her hand covered his mouth. "Quiet."

"Fake Ploeg," he whispered. "He was with the police. A dirty collaborator."

"Did you see him?" she asked softly. "Was he really dead?"

Anton nodded. He realized that she could not see him, could at most feel him, and said: "As a doornail." Once more the bloodstains in the snow were there in front of his eyes. "I'm in his son's class. He's also called Fake."

He heard her take a deep breath.

"You know," she said after a while, "if those Underground people hadn't done this, Ploeg would have murdered many more, and then . . ."

She pulled her arm away and began to sob. It frightened Anton; he wanted to comfort her but didn't know how. He sat up and carefully reached out till he felt her hair: thick, springy hair.

"Why are you crying?"

She took his hand and pressed it against her heart.

"It's all so horrible," she said in a choking voice. "The world is hell, hell. I'm glad it's almost over now, I can't take it anymore . . ."

Under the palm of his hand he felt her soft breast, a strange softness such as he had never felt before, but he didn't dare remove his hand.

"What's almost over?"

She took his hand in hers. From her voice he could tell that she had turned to face him.

"The War, the War, of course. Just a few more weeks and it'll all be over. The Americans are at the Rhine and the Russians at the Oder."

"For sure? How do you know?"

She had said it with total conviction, whereas at home he had only heard vague rumors that seemed to promise one thing and then turned out to mean another. She didn't answer. Though the strip of light under the door was very faint, now he could just see the outline of her head and body, her loose, somewhat wild mass of hair, the place where she sat, an arm approaching him.

"Do you mind if I touch your face so I can make out what you look like?"

Softly her cold fingertips caressed his forehead, his eyebrows, cheeks, nose, and lips. He sat motionless, his head slightly tilted back. He felt that this was something very solemn, a kind of initiation, something they might do in Africa. All of a sudden she pulled her hand back and moaned.

"What's the matter?" he asked, frightened.

"Nothing . . . Never mind." Now she sat bent over.

"Do you hurt?"

"Really, it's nothing. Honest!" She straightened and said, "A few weeks ago I was in an even darker place than this."

"Do you live in Heemstede?"

"Don't ask. It's better for you not to know a thing about me. You'll understand later. All right?"

"Sure."

"Then listen. Tonight there's no moon, and yet it's very bright, but that time it was cloudy and there was no snow yet. I had gone to visit a friend in my neighborhood and we sat and talked. I didn't leave him till the middle of the night, long after curfew. It was so dark that no one would be able to see me. I know the neighborhood by heart and walked home feeling my way along the walls and fences. I couldn't see a thing. I might as well have had no eyes. I had taken off my shoes so as not to make any noise. I really saw absolutely nothing, but all along I knew exactly where I was. At least, so I thought. I visualized everything in my memory, I had walked along here at least a thousand times, I knew every corner, every hedge, every tree, every stoop—everything.

"And suddenly I lost it. Nothing fitted anymore. I felt a

bush where there should have been a windowsill, a lamp-post where there ought to be a garage exit. I took a few more steps and couldn't feel anything more. I was still standing on the cobblestones, but I knew that a moat was somewhere near, and I was afraid I might fall into it if I took another step. I crept around on hands and knees for a while. I didn't have any matches or a cigarette lighter. Finally I just sat down and waited for dawn. Can you imagine how alone I felt?"

"Did you cry?" asked Anton, and held his breath. It was as if here in the pitch dark, he could see whatever had been invisible then, too.

"Not exactly," she said with a laugh. "But I was scared, believe me! Perhaps even more by the silence than by the darkness. I knew that there were lots of people all about, but everything had disappeared. The world stopped at my skin. My fear had nothing to do with the War anymore. Besides, I was terribly cold."

"And then?"

"What do you suppose? I was sitting on the street right in front of my own house. Just imagine! In five steps I was home."

"Something like that happened to me once!" said Anton, who had completely forgotten where he was, and why. "When I was staying with my uncle in Amsterdam."

"That must have been some time ago?"

"Last summer, when the trains were still running. I think I'd had a bad dream; I woke up and wanted to go to the bathroom. It was pitch-black. At home I always step out of my bed on the left side, you know, but here there was suddenly a wall. On my right, where the wall usually is, there wasn't anything. I was scared stiff. It was as if the wall was much harder and thicker than an ordinary wall, and on the other side where there was no wall, it seemed like a canyon."

"And then did you cry?"

"Sure, of course. What else!"

"And then your aunt or your uncle turned on the light, and you remembered where you were."

"Yes, my uncle did. I was sitting up in bed and . . ."

"Sh!"

Steps came down the stairs. She put her arm around him again and listened, motionless. Voices in the hall, a rattle of keys. Briefly there was a sound that Anton could not identify, then a sudden cursing and the dull thud of a beating. Someone was being dragged along the hall, while someone else was left swearing in the cell. With a loud iron clang the door fell closed. In the hall the man was being beaten or kicked; he screamed. More boots came pounding down the stairs, more screaming, after which it sounded as if the man was being dragged upstairs. It grew quiet. Someone laughed. They heard nothing more.

Anton was trembling.

"Who was that?" he asked.

"I don't know. I haven't been here long either. Those bastards . . . Thank God they'll all end up on the gallows, and sooner than you think. Believe me, the Russians and the Americans will make short shrift of them. Let's think about something else," she said, turning toward him and stroking his hair with both hands, "while we still can."

"What do you mean?"

"Well, while they still leave us together in here. Tomorrow they'll let you go."

"And you?"

"Maybe not," she said, as if there were a possibility that tomorrow they might set her free also. "But with me, too, everything will be all right in the end; don't worry. What shall we talk about? Or are you tired? Do you want to sleep?"

"Not me."

"Good. We've been talking all the time about the dark; shall we talk about light?"

"Fine."

"Just imagine, lots of light. Sun. Summer. What else?"

"The beach."

"Yes, before it was full of bunkers and barricades. The dunes. The sun shining in a dune hollow. Do you remember how blinding that could be?"

"You bet I do. And how! The branches lying in there were always bleached by the sun."

Suddenly, without transition, she began to talk as if to a third person in the cell.

"Light, yes, but light is not always just light. I mean, some time ago I wanted to write a poem comparing light to love—no, I mean love to light. Yes, that's another possibility, of course. You could also compare light to love. Maybe that's even more beautiful, for light is older than love. Christians say it's not so, but then, they're Christians. Or are you a Christian?"

"I don't really think so."

"In the poem I wanted to compare love to the kind of light you sometimes see clinging to trees right after a sunset: the magical sort of light. That's the kind of light people have inside them when they're in love with someone. Hate is the darkness, that's no good. And yet we've got to hate Fascists, and that's considered perfectly all right. How is that possible? It's because we hate them in the name of the light, I guess, whereas they hate only in the name of darkness. We hate hate itself, and for this reason our hate is better than theirs.

"But that's why it's more difficult for us. For them everything is very simple, but for us it's more complicated. We've got to become a little bit like them in order to fight them— so we become a little bit unlike ourselves. But they don't have that problem; they can do away with us without any qualms. We first have to do away with something inside ourselves before we can do away with them. Not them; they can simply remain themselves, that's why they're so strong. But they'll lose in the end, because they have no light in them. The only thing is, we mustn't become too much like them, mustn't destroy ourselves altogether, otherwise they'll have won in the end . . ."

She gave a brief moan. Before he could speak, she continued. He didn't understand a word she was saying, but he was flattered that she should be talking to him as to a grown-up.

"And there's something else about that kind of light. Whenever someone is in love with someone else, they always say that the person they love is very beautiful, physically or mentally, or both. Often other people can't see this at all, and they're usually right. But when people are in love they're always beautiful, for in loving they are lit up by the light. There's a man who loves me and finds me very beautiful, which I'm not at all, really. He's the beautiful one, even though in many ways he's terribly ugly. And I'm beautiful too, but only because I'm in love with him, though he doesn't know it. He thinks I'm not, but I do love him. Now you're the only one who knows it, even though you don't know who I am and who he is. He has a wife and two children about your age. They need him, just as you need your father and mother . . ."

Suddenly she was silent.

"Where do you suppose my father and mother are?" Anton asked softly.

"They're probably locked up too, somewhere. I'm sure you'll see them tomorrow."

"But why are they in another place than I am?"

"Why indeed! Because we're dealing with monsters. And because the whole thing is a big heap of ruins; the Krauts are just keeping busy. They're shitting in their pants at the moment. But don't you worry. I'm much more concerned about your brother."

"As he ran away, he picked up Ploeg's gun," Anton said, hoping this would not strike her as too terrible.

A few seconds went by before she said, "For Christ's sake."

He could tell by her voice that this was somehow fatal. What had happened to Peter? Suddenly he could take no more. He slumped against her and instantly fell sound asleep.

4

He was awakened half an hour or an hour later by the shouting that had echoed throughout Europe for years. Right away another flashlight blinded him. He was grabbed by the arm and pulled off the cot and down the hall so fast that he never saw his cell mate again. Germans and policemen were still standing all over the place. An important SS man with a skull on his cap and silver stars and stripes on his collar slammed the cell door shut. He was a handsome man of about thirty-five with the kind of regular, noble features that Anton had often seen in boys' book illustrations.

To lock up such a young boy, he shouted as he climbed the stairs, and with that terrorist, yet! Had everyone lost their minds? That blasted Communist female didn't belong here either, he would take her with him to Amsterdam, to his office on Euterpe Street. It was lucky she hadn't been freed yet, or some of the officials in this place wouldn't have survived either. What kind of pigsty was this? Who had given the orders? What? Someone from the Security Service! *Et tu, Brute*! Probably another one of those two-faced operators getting into position for the next time around, making himself out to be Santa Claus, the great ally of the Resistance. That will be of enormous interest to the Gestapo. This boy is lucky he is still alive. How did he get blood on his face?

Once more Anton was standing in the waiting room with a gloved finger pointing at him. Blood? He touched his cheeks. A cop pointed to a round shaving glass hanging from one of the steel braces against the wall. He stood on tiptoe and in the magnifying mirror saw the bloody, dried traces of her fingers on his white face and in his hair.

"That's not mine."

So then it was hers! exclaimed the officer. That's the limit. She's been wounded, get a doctor here at once, he still needed her. As far as the boy goes, take him to the Ortskommandantur, the Regional Command, for the night so he can be handed over to his family tomorrow. And be quick about it, *bisschen Ruck-Zuck*, you bunch of cheeseheads. No wonder they're getting themselves mowed down at the drop of a hat. Chief Inspector Ploeg! Had to go for a little bike ride in the dark, the idiot.

Wrapped in a horse blanket, Anton was taken outside by a helmeted German. The night was still crystal clear. In front of the door stood a Mercedes belonging, of course, to the officer, with a convertible linen roof and big compressors next to the hood.

The German had a carbine on his back, and the tails of his dark-gray coat were tied around his legs, so that he walked with the wide-legged, ungainly tread of a bear. He told Anton to sit behind him on the motorcycle and hold on tight. Anton hitched up the blanket, embraced the huge shoulders, and clung with his torso to the man's gun-strapped back.

Weaving and skidding, they drove off beneath the stars through the abandoned streets to Haarlem, a ride of less than ten minutes. The snow crunched beneath the tires, but it seemed as if not even the sputtering of the motor could disturb the silence. So now here he was, riding a motorcycle for the first time in his life. In spite of the cold he had to make an effort not to drop off to sleep again. It was dark and light at the same time. The neck of the German in front of his eyes was a strip of skin with short, dark hair between the rubber collar of the coat and the steel of the helmet. Anton was thinking of something that had happened a year ago, at the indoor swimming pool. It was supposed to be evacuated at a certain hour for the Wehrmacht, but he had dawdled so long in his dressing room that he was too late. Outside he heard singing and the stamping of boots as the regiment approached. "Hei li, hei lo, hei la!" A little later the soldiers, laughing and whooping, thundered into the silent bathhouse. He didn't hear any of the dressing-room doors opening; they were stripping in the communal area. A minute later their naked feet splashed in the direction of the swimming pool. When everything had quieted down, he summoned the courage to slip out. Suddenly he saw them at the end of the hall behind the glass doors. Inexplicably, they had changed into human beings, just ordinary men, all naked, white bodies with brown faces and necks, arms that were brown up to the elbows. He left in a hurry. He saw the abandoned uniforms hanging in the dressing room, the caps, the belts, the boots. Such menace there, all that violence at rest . . . With the weightless suspension of sleepwalkers rising from their beds, the uniforms now detach themselves from their hooks and float toward a burning pile of firewood, tall flames licking the porch of a white country house—but luckily everything is underwater, in a canal or a swimming pool; the flames hiss as they go out . . .

He woke up with a start. They had come to a standstill in the Hout, at the entrance to the trench that had been dug around the Ortskommandantur. Everywhere he saw barbed wire. A sentry let them pass. In the dark courtyard there was a coming and going of trucks and cars. Their headlights were shielded with little visors, and the glass was blacked out except for narrow horizontal strips. The racket of motors and horns made a strange contrast to this careful control of lights.

The soldier set the motorcycle on its kickstand and took

Anton inside. Here too there was unbroken activity: the back-and-forth traffic of military men, telephones ringing, typewriters clattering. He had to wait on a wooden bench in a small, heated room. Through the open door he could look into a long hall—and there he suddenly saw Mr. Korteweg. He came out of one door, crossed the hall, and disappeared through the opposite door, accompanied by a hatless soldier carrying papers under one arm. No doubt they already knew what he and his daughter had done, moving that body. At the thought that his parents too were probably here somewhere, Anton yawned, keeled over sideways, and fell asleep.

When he woke up, he was looking into the eyes of a rather elderly sergeant in a sloppy uniform and calf-length boots that were too wide, who gave him a friendly nod. Anton was lying in another room under a woolen blanket on a red sofa. Outside it was daylight. Anton smiled back. Awareness that his house no longer existed came briefly but vanished at once. The sergeant pulled up a chair. On its seat he set down a tin cup of warm milk and a plate with three large, oblong, dark-brown sandwiches spread with something the color of frosted glass. Years later, as he traveled through Germany to his house in Tuscany, Anton learned that this was goose fat: *Schmaltz*. Never again would anything taste as good. Not even the most expensive dinners in the best restaurants in the world, at Bocuse's in Lyon, or Lasserre in Paris, where he would stop on the way back from Italy. Nor could the most expensive Lafite Rothschild or Chambertin ever compare to that warm milk back then. A man who has never been hungry may possess a more refined palate, but he has no idea what it means to eat.

"Tastes good? *Schmeckt?*" said the sergeant. After he had fetched another cup of milk and watched, amused, as this one too was gulped down, Anton had to wash up at a faucet in the toilet. In the mirror he could see that the blood smears on his face had become rust-brown. Hesitantly, bit by bit, he removed the only trace left of her. After that he was ushered into the Ortskommandant's room, an arm encircling his shoulders. He hesitated at the threshold, but the sergeant pointed him to the armchair facing the desk.

The Ortskommandant, the military governor of the city, was on the telephone and looked at him briefly, without actually seeing him, but with a reassuring, fatherly nod. A short, fat man with short-cropped gray hair, he wore the gray uniform of the Wehrmacht. His holster with the pistol in it lay next to his hat on the desk, near four framed photographs, of which Anton could only see the backs, resting on little triangular holders. On the opposite wall hung a portrait of Hitler. Anton looked out the window at the bare, ice-coated, immovable trees that were totally unaware of what wartime was all about. The Ortskommandant hung the receiver on the hook, made a note, searched for something among his papers, then folded his hands on the blotter and asked if Anton had slept well. He spoke Dutch with a heavy accent, but quite clearly.

"Yes sir," said Anton.

"It is dreadful what all happened yesterday." The Ortskommandant shook his head for a while. "The world is a *Jammertal*, a valley of tears. Everywhere it is the same. My house in Linz was bombed also. Everything kaput. *Kinder* dead." Nodding, he kept looking at Anton. "You want to say something, don't you? Go ahead."

"Are my father and mother here, maybe? They were also taken away yesterday." He knew that he mustn't mention Peter, because that might set them on his trail.

The Ortskommandant once more began to shuffle papers. "That was another assignment. Sorry, I can do nothing about it. Everything is momentarily mixed up. I think they are somewhere near here. Dat we must wait and see. The War can *ja überhaupt*, not last much longer. Then this *alles* will have been a bad dream. *Na,*" he said with a sudden laugh and reached out with both arms toward Anton. "What we do now *mit* you? You stay by us? Will you be a soldier?"

Anton smiled too and did not know what to say.

"What you want to be when you grow up . . ." He glanced briefly at a small gray card, his identity card, Anton realized. "Anton Emanuel Willem Steenwijk?"

"I don't know yet. Pilot, perhaps."

The Ortskommandant smiled, but his smile vanished almost at once.

"So," he said, and unscrewed his thick orange fountain pen. "Now let's get down to business. Do you have family in Haarlem?"

"No sir."

The Ortskommandant looked up. "No family at all?"

"Only in Amsterdam. My uncle and aunt."

"You think can you stay *da* awhile?"

"Oh yes."

"What's this uncle's name?"

"Van Liempt."

"First name?"

"Eh . . . Peter."

"Profession?"

"Doctor."

He was pleased at the idea of staying with his aunt and uncle for a while. He often thought of their beautiful house on the Apollolaan; it had an air of mystery for him, perhaps because of the big city all around it.

While the Ortskommandant took down the address, he said in a solemn voice, "Phoebus Apollo, the god of light and beauty." Suddenly he looked at his watch, put down his pen, and stood up. "Just a moment," he said and left the room in a hurry. In the hall he called out something to a soldier, who thundered off. "In a while a small convoy is leaving for Amsterdam," he said as he returned. "You can go right along. Schulz!" he called. This was apparently the sergeant's name. He was to accompany Anton to Amsterdam.

The Ortskommandant himself would quickly write a *Notiz* to those in charge over there; in the meantime the boy should be dressed warmly. He went to Anton, shook his hand, and laid the other hand on his shoulder. "Have a safe trip, *Herr Fliegergeneral*. And be very brave."

"Yes sir. Good day, sir."

"At your service, little one."

Anton was pinched on the cheek by index and middle finger; then the sergeant led him out of the office. Talking all the while in a dialect Anton couldn't understand a word of, Schulz took him to a stuffy storeroom. There were long rows of soldiers' coats and boots, and on the shelves, rows of helmets. Schulz pulled out two thick gray sweaters and made Anton wear one on top of the other. He tied a scarf around Anton's head and put the heavy helmet on top. When it sank wobbling over his ears, Schulz stuffed paper behind the leather lining and pulled the straps tight, after which it fit somewhat better. The sergeant stood back, looked him over, and shook his head, dissatisfied. Pulling a coat from the left end of the row, he held it up to Anton, then took a huge pair of scissors out of a drawer and laid the coat on the floor. Anton watched wide-eyed as Schulz simply cut the garment down to size, slashing wide strips off the bottom and the sleeves. Anton slipped his arms into them, and Schulz tied a raveling piece of rope around his middle to keep everything in place. Finally Schulz gave him a big pair of lined gloves, after which he burst out laughing, said something unintelligible, and laughed still louder.

If only his schoolmates could see him now! But they were probably all at home, bored stiff, with no idea of what was happening to him. Upstairs Schulz put on a helmet himself. After he had picked up the letter at the Ortskommandant's and stuffed it in his pocket, they left the building.

Thin needles of glistening ice fell out of the dark sky. The small convoy stood waiting at the garage across from the fenced-off area, four high transport trucks covered with gray canvas, and in the lead a long, open car. On the front seat next to the driver sat an officer impatiently waiting for them. On the two seats behind were four soldiers muffled in heavy clothes, machine guns in their laps. Anton had to climb into the cabin of the first truck and sit between Schulz and a gruff soldier at the wheel. Such a lot was happening! For Anton, who was still too young to absorb the past, each new event erased the preceding one from awareness and buried it in his subconscious.

They left Haarlem, driving through the suburbs, and came to the long, straight, two-lane highway that ran along the old ship canal to Amsterdam. On the left the overhead wiring of the electric train and the trolley hung to the ground in graceful curves. Here and there the rails stood upright like the horns of a snail. Sometimes even the poles were lying down. On all sides, the hard frozen ground. They drove slowly. It was impossible to hold a conversation because of the racket inside the cabin. Everything was made of dirty, rattling steel, which somehow told him more about the War than he had ever understood before. Fire and this steel—that was the War.

Without meeting anyone they drove through Halfweg, along the abandoned sugar factory, and came to the final stretch of the twenty kilometers to Amsterdam. He could already see the city at the horizon, behind the sandy embankment laid out, as his father had explained to him, for a projected ring highway. They were driving along snowed-in peat diggings, when the front car suddenly swerved sharply into the embankment. The soldiers waved their arms, shouted, and jumped out of the trucks. At that moment Anton too saw the plane. No larger than a fly, it flew at a right angle across the road. The driver of his truck stepped on the brakes, crying, "Get out!" and jumped down himself without turning off the motor. Schulz did the same on the other side. All about him Anton heard shouting. The men in front crouched behind their car clutching their machine guns, ready to shoot. Out of the corner of his eye he saw someone calling him, waving. It was Schulz, but Anton could not take his eyes off the small thing that circled over the road and then came straight at him, growing fast. It was a Spitfire; no, a Mosquito; no, a Spitfire. Mesmerized, he stared at the shaky steel that approached as if it loved him. It could not harm him. He was, after all, on their side, they knew that, of course—even yesterday. From below the wings he saw some flashes crackle, minor incidents, hardly worth noticing. On the ground too, fire broke loose. It whistled and popped and rattled on all sides. He felt the blows of the impact, and because he thought the plane would ram into him, he dove below the dashboard while the motor bellowed above him like a steam roller.

A second later he was pulled out from his hiding place under the steering wheel and dragged to the ditch. To the left and right of the road he saw at least a hundred soldiers rising. Farther on, near the last truck, he heard the wounded moaning. When the plane disappeared into the clouds and it became evident that it would not return, Anton, his heart still pounding, crossed the road to join the sergeant. Ice splinters as large as gramophone needles blew into his face. On the other side of the truck, right near the running board, two soldiers carefully turned a body over. It was Schulz. The side of his chest had become a dark pool of blood and tatters. Blood was also coming out of his nose and mouth. He was still alive, but his face was contorted with such pain that Anton felt the need to do something at once to relieve it. Suddenly he turned away, nauseated and in a cold sweat, less from the sight of all the blood than from the frustration. He pushed the helmet off his head, loosened the scarf, and groped for the shaking hood of the truck as the vomit spouted out of his wide-open throat. At almost that instant the last truck in the column burst into flame.

He hardly noticed what happened next. The helmet was being shoved back onto his head and someone took him to the open car. The officer shouted commands; Schulz and the other wounded, and probably dead, were laid out in the third truck. All the other soldiers had to pile into the second one. A few minutes later the convoy was back on the road, leaving the burning truck behind.

As Amsterdam approached, the officer kept shouting past him at the driver. Suddenly he asked Anton who the hell he was anyway, *verfluchtnochmal*, and where was he supposed to be going? Anton understood, but he was breathing so convulsively that he couldn't answer. The officer gestured as if to throw something away and said he didn't give a shit, *scheissegal*. Anton kept seeing Schulz's face. He had been lying right next to the truck; he had wanted to pull Anton out to safety. It was all Anton's fault, and now Schulz would surely die.

They drove into the city through a gap in the embankment. A bit farther on, the officer stood up at a street corner and waved the drivers of the first two trucks straight ahead (briefly Anton caught a glimpse of his own vomit on the hood of the first one), after which he motioned to the third to follow him. For a while they drove along a wide canal that was practically deserted. Now and then they crossed a street where groups of women and children in rags poked around for something between the rusty trolley rails where the stones had been removed. Through narrow, silent streets with dilapidated houses they reached the gate of the Western Hospital. Inside, the hospital was a city in itself, with its own streets and large buildings. They came to a halt near an emergency shed with an arrow saying *Lazarett*. Immediately several nurses ran out. They dressed quite differently from Karin Korteweg, for they wore dark coats down to their ankles and much smaller white caps that enclosed their hair like snoods. The officer and the men on the back seat stepped out of the car. But when Anton wanted to follow, the driver held him back.

The two of them drove alone into the city. Anton looked about with a leaden weight in his head. After a few minutes they passed behind the Rijksmuseum, which he had visited with his father, and came into a wide square with its center fenced off. Here stood two huge, rectangular bunkers. At the opposite side of the square, right across from the Rijksmuseum, was a building shaped like a Greek temple, with a lyre on the roof. *Concertgebouw* was written in big letters under the tympanum. In front of this building was a low structure bearing the sign *Wehrmachtheim Erika*. Several of the large, free-standing villas to the right and left clearly had been taken over by the Germans. The car stopped at one of these. A sentinel with a gun over his shoulder looked at Anton and asked the driver if this was the latest recruit.

In the hall too they laughed at him, the little boy with his helmet and oversized coat, but soon an officer who was about to climb the stairs put an end to their teasing. He wore shiny high boots and all kinds of braid and badges and ribbons, and around his neck hung the Iron Cross. Perhaps he was actually a general. He came to a stop, four younger officers remaining a few steps behind him, and asked what was going on. Anton could not understand what the driver, who had snapped to attention, answered, but clearly it was about the plane attack. As he listened, the general took a flat Egyptian cigarette out of a package and tapped it on the lid, where Anton read Stanbul. One of the young officers instantly offered a match. He tipped his head back briefly, blew the smoke straight up in the air, and dismissed the driver with a wave of the hand. Anton had to follow him up the stairs with the four young officers, who laughed and whispered among themselves. The general's back, straight as a ramrod, leaned forward in at least a twenty-degree angle.

They came to a large room. With an irritated gesture he ordered Anton to remove those ridiculous garments. Anton looked like a ragamuffin from the ghetto of Bialystok, he said, at which the officers smiled. Anton did what he was told, and the general opened a door and snarled something into a side room. The younger officers remained in the background; one sat down elegantly in the window seat and lit a cigarette.

As Anton took a chair in front of the desk, a pretty, slender girl in a black dress entered. Her blond hair was pinned up on the sides but hung down in the back. She set a cup of coffee with milk in front of him; on the saucer lay a piece of milk chocolate.

"Here you are," she said in Dutch. "I bet you like that."

Chocolate! Only by hearsay did he know that it still existed. This was very like paradise. But he wasn't given a chance to taste it, for the general wanted to hear what had happened from beginning to end. The girl functioned as interpreter. The first part of his story, about the assault and the fire, made Anton cry a little (but it was so long ago by now). The general listened unmoved, however, now carefully stroking his smoothly brushed hair with the palm of his hand, now caressing his smooth, shiny jaw with the back of his fingers. But as the story proceeded, he seemed unable to believe his ears. "*Na, so was!*" he exclaimed when he heard that Anton had been locked in a cell below a police station. "This is incredible!" Anton kept it a secret that someone else had been in there too. That he should have been brought to the Ortskommandantur afterwards the general said was unheard-of. "*Unerhört!*" Weren't there any homes for children in Haarlem? The Ortskommandantur! That was really the limit. And the Ortskommandant had sent him to Amsterdam with a military convoy? When he knew perfectly well there were strafers everywhere? Had they all gone crazy in Haarlem? It boggled the mind. "It has all been a series of ridiculous mistakes!" He raised his arms and let them fall flat-handed onto the desk. The officer in the window seat burst out laughing at his colorful indignation, and the general then said, "You may laugh all you like." Had the gentlemen in Haarlem had the courtesy to give Anton any messages? His papers, for instance, just to name an example?

"Yes," said Anton. But in a flash he saw the sergeant stuff the letter into his inside pocket, the very spot where the dreadful wound had opened half an hour later.

When he began to cry again, the general stood up, annoyed. Take him away and calm him down and call Haarlem at once. Or not, after all. Let them stew in their own juice. Call the uncle and have him pick up the boy.

The girl put a hand on his shoulder and led him out.

When his uncle appeared an hour later, he was still sobbing in a waiting room. The corners of his mouth were brown with chocolate, and on his lap a copy of *Signal* lay open at a dramatic drawing of air combat. Van Liempt threw it to the ground, knelt in front of him, and silently held him close. Then he stood up and said, "Come, Anton, let's get out of here." Anton looked up at him and saw his mother's eyes.

"Did you hear what happened, Uncle Peter?"

"Yes."

"I have a coat somewhere . . ."

"Let's get out of here." Holding onto Van Liempt's hand, without a coat but wearing the two sweaters, he walked out into the winter day. He was sobbing but hardly knew why, as if his memories had washed away his tears. His other hand felt cold. He stuck it into his pocket, where he touched something he could not place. He looked: it was one of the dice.

SECOND EPISODE

1952

1

All the rest is a postscript—the cloud of ash that rises from the volcano, circles around the earth, and continues to rain down on all its continents for years.

In May, a few days after the Liberation, having received no news yet of Anton's parents and Peter, Van Liempt left early in the morning for Haarlem to try and find out what had happened. Apparently they had been kept under arrest, though this was not customary during such reprisals. But even if they had been taken to a concentration camp in Vught or Amersfoort, they should have been freed by now. Only the survivors of the German camps had not yet returned home.

That afternoon Anton went into town with his aunt. Amsterdam looked like a dying man who suddenly flushes, opens his eyes, and miraculously comes back to life. Everywhere flags at windowsills in need of paint, everywhere music and dancing and crowds rejoicing in the streets where grass and thistles grew between the pavement. Pale, starved people laughingly crowded about fat Canadians wearing berets instead of caps, dressed not in gray, black, or green, but in beige or light-brown uniforms that did not encase them tightly like armor, but hung loose and easy, like peacetime clothes, showing hardly any difference between soldiers and officers. Jeeps and armored cars were being patted like holy objects. Whoever could speak English not only became part of the heavenly kingdom that had come down to earth, but perhaps even received a cigarette. Boys his own age sat triumphantly on top of car radiators marked with white stars surrounded by circles. Yet he himself did not take part. Not because he was worried about his parents or Peter, for he never thought about that, but more because none of this celebration was really a part of him or ever would be. His entire universe had become that other night-marish one which now fortunately had come to an end, and about which he never wanted to think again. Nevertheless it was part of him, so that all in all, he didn't have much left.

At dinner time they returned home and he went to his room, where he was quite comfortable by now. His uncle and aunt were childless and treated him as if he were their own son—or really with more consideration and less friction than if he actually had been their real child. At times he wondered what it would be like to go back to live with his parents in Haarlem, and this thought confused him so much that he quickly put it aside. He liked being at his aunt and uncle's house on the Apollolaan precisely because he did not feel like their son.

His uncle had the habit of always knocking before he entered. When Anton looked at his face, he saw at once the news he had brought. The steel clamp that had protected his uncle's pants leg on the bicycle was still around his left ankle. He sat on the desk chair and told Anton to be prepared for very sad news. His father and mother had never gone to prison. They had been shot that night, along with the twenty-nine hostages. Nobody knew what had become of Peter, so there was still hope for him. His uncle had been to the police, but they didn't know about anyone except the hostages. Then he had gone to the neighbors on the quay. No one was home at the Aartses' in Bide-a-Wee. The Kortewegs were home but refused to receive him. Finally it was the Beumers who told him the news. Mr. Beumer had seen it. Van Liempt did not go into details: Anton did not ask for any. He sat on his bed with the wall on the left, and stared down at the flamelike shapes in the gray linoleum.

He had the feeling that he had known it all along. His uncle told him that the Beumers were very glad to hear he was still alive. Van Liempt pulled the clamp off his ankle and held it in his hand. It had the shape of a horseshoe. Of course, he said, Anton would continue to live here.

Not till June did they learn that Peter too had been shot on that same evening. By then it seemed like a message from prehistoric times, hard to imagine. For Anton that distance of five months between January and June, 1945, was incomparably longer than the distance between June of 1945 and the present day. It was on this distortion of time that he later blamed his inability to explain to his children what the War had been like. His family had escaped from his memory, had retreated to a forgotten region of which he had only brief and random glimpses—as when he looked out of the window in school, or out of the rear platform on the trolley car—a dark region of cold and hunger and shooting, blood, flames, shouts, prison cells, hermetically sealed somewhere deep inside him. At such moments it was if he remembered a dream, but not so much what the dream had been about, as simply the fact that it had been a nightmare. Yet at the core of that hermetic darkness now and then flashed a single source of blinding light: the fingertips of the girl caressing his face. Whether she had had anything to do with the assault, and what had happened to her, he did not know. He had no desire to know.

He finished the gymnasium as a fair to middling student and went on to medical school. By then a lot had been published about the Occupation, but he didn't bother to read any of it, or any of the novels and stories about those days. Nor did he go to the State Institute for War Information, where he might have found out all that was known about the death of Fake Ploeg, and exactly how Peter had met his death. The family of which he had been a member had been exterminated once and for all; it was enough to be aware of this. All he knew was that the assault had never been brought to trial, for in that case he would have been questioned.

And the German man with the scar in the long coat had never been tracked down. (But perhaps he had already been removed by the Gestapo. Never mind; he is the least important character in this drama.) He must have acted more or less on his own initiative. To set houses on fire in places where Nazis had been shot was not unusual, but to execute the inhabitants as well—that kind of terror had been practiced only in Poland and Russia. In those countries, however, Anton would have been killed too, even if he had still been in the cradle.

2

But things don't vanish all that easily. In September, 1952, while he was in his second year of medical school, a fellow student invited him to a birthday party in Haarlem. He had not been back since he left seven years before with the German convoy. At first he didn't plan to go, yet all day he kept thinking about it. Suddenly after lunch he grabbed a novel by a young Haarlem writer that would do for a present, though he had actually meant to read it himself, and took the trolley to the station. He felt like someone going to a whorehouse for the first time.

Beyond the sandy embankment, the train passed under a huge steel pipe that was vomiting a thick, steel-gray mud onto the former peat diggings on the other side of the street. The burned-out truck had been removed. He watched the traffic on the street, his chin resting in the palm of his hand. The trolley too was running again. As he passed Halfweg he saw the silhouette of Haarlem, still very much the way Ruysdael painted it—although in those days there were woods and fields where laundry lay bleaching, where Anton's house later stood. But the sky was the same: massive Alps of clouds with beams of light leaning against them. What he saw was not just any city like so many others in the world. It was as different as he himself was from other people.

Anyone watching him sitting on the pale wooden bench in third class, peering out of the compartment window of a train confiscated from the Reichsbahn, would see a twenty-year-old with sleek, dark hair that kept falling over his forehead, which he would toss back with a brief movement of the head. For some reason this gesture was attractive, perhaps because it was repeated so often that it implied a certain amount of patience. He had dark eyebrows and a smooth, nut-colored complexion, somewhat darker around the eyes. He wore gray slacks, a heavy blue blazer, a club tie, and a shirt whose pointed collar tips turned upward. The smoke that he blew with pursed lips at the windowpane clung to the glass in a thin mist for a moment.

He took the trolley to his friend's house. The friend too lived in Haarlem South, but since his family hadn't moved there till after the war, they wouldn't question Anton about the past. When the trolley swerved into the Hout, he caught sight for a minute of the former Ortskommandantur. The trench and barbed wire had disappeared; there was nothing left but a dilapidated abandoned hotel, its windows nailed shut. The garage (a restaurant before the War) was now in ruins. Probably his friend had no idea what kind of establishment this had once been.

"So you came after all," he said as he opened the door.

"Sorry I'm late."

"Never mind. Did you have trouble finding it?"

"Not really."

In the garden behind the house a long table stood under the tall trees. It held potato salad and other delicacies, bottles, stacks of plates, silver. On another table were the presents, to which Anton added his book. The guests stood and sat about the lawn. After he had been introduced to everyone, he joined the slightly inebriated group that he knew from Amsterdam. Holding their glasses of beer in front of their chests, they formed a circle by the edge of the water. Like Anton, they wore blazers that hung loose on their boyish frames. The leader of the group was his friend's older brother, a dentistry student in Utrecht, who wore a huge, shapeless black shoe on his right foot.

He was holding forth: "The fact is, you're all softies; that's natural. All you've got on your minds, except for jerking off, of course, is how to avoid the draft."

"That's easy for you to say, Gerrit Jan. They obviously don't want you, with that paw of yours."

"Well, I'll tell you something else, you jerk. If you had one ounce of guts, you'd not only join the army, but volunteer to go to Korea. None of you have any idea what's going on over there. The barbarians are storming the gates of Christian civilization." He wagged his index finger at them. "Compared to them, the Fascists were mere boys. Just read Koestler."

"Why don't you go yourself? Kick in their brains with that ridiculous shoe of yours, Quasimodo."

"Touché!" Gerrit Jan laughed.

"Korea is getting to be just like the University of Amsterdam," commented another. "A haven for misfits."

"Gentlemen," said Gerrit Jan, raising his glass, "let's drink to the downfall of Red Fascism, at home and abroad."

"I do keep thinking I should have joined," said a boy who hadn't picked up the drift of the conversation. "But apparently there are lots of former SS-ers in the army. I heard that if they enlist, they get off scot-free."

"So what? There's more in it than that for the SS-ers. In Korea they can really get ahead."

Get ahead, thought Anton. Really get ahead. Between two boys he peered at the opposite shore of the pond, at the peaceful lanes where people bicycled and someone was taking a dog out. Villas were there, too. Somewhat beyond them, though not visible from here, was the nursery school where he used to stand in line at the central kitchen. A bit farther and toward the left, behind the vacant lots, was the place where it had all happened. He shouldn't have come; he should never have returned to Haarlem. He should have buried all that, the way one buries the dead.

"A certain dreamer is peering into the distance," said Gerrit Jan, and when Anton looked up at him, "Yes, you, Steenwijk. Well, what's your opinion?"

"What do you mean?"

"Are we going to face up to the Communists, or are we going to pussyfoot around them?"

"I've had my share," said Anton.

At that moment someone started a record on the veranda: "Thanks for the memory . . ." He smiled at the coincidence, but when he saw that the others hadn't noticed, shrugged briefly and walked away from them. The music blended with the dappled shade below the trees and somehow stirred up his memories. He was in Haarlem. It was a warm autumn day, perhaps the last one of the year, and he was once more in Haarlem. This was all wrong, and he resolved never to come back again, even if he were offered a job here at a hundred thousand gulden a year. But since he happened to be here, he wanted to say goodbye once and for all—now, immediately.

"And you, young man?"

Startled, he looked up into the face of his host. A short man with gray hair brushed to the side, wearing an ill-fitting suit with pants too short for him, as was the fashion with a certain element of the Dutch upper classes. Beside him stood his wife, a refined lady with a crooked back, so frail, all in white, that she looked as if at any moment she might fly away in a puff of dust.

"Yes, Mr. Van Lennep," he said with a smile, although he had no idea what the question was.

"Are you having fun?"

"I'm doing my best."

"Good for you. Though you don't look very happy, my friend."

"Yes," he said. "I think I'll take a tour around the block. Please don't mind me."

"Oh, we don't mind anything. Free and easy. Go ahead and stretch your legs, it clears the head."

Between tea-drinking family members sitting in white garden chairs, he found his way into the house and out to the street. He turned into a side street and walked along the pond. When he had crossed to the other side, he looked back at the party on the lawn. The music that drifted over the water sounded even louder from here. At that moment Gerrit Jan noticed him.

"Hey, over there, Steenwijk, you asshole. The recruiting office is in the other direction."

With a wave of his hand Anton let him know that he got the joke. After that he did not look back again.

He didn't take the path across the lots, but went along the street which, around the bend, turned into the quay. This was all wrong, what he was doing; it was a mistake. "The criminal returns to the scene of the crime." With sudden excitement he recognized the herringbone pattern of the brick pavement. He had never noticed it in the old days, but now he saw it and realized that it had always been there. When he came to the water, he kept his eyes focused on the other side. The farmhands' cottages, the little farms, the mill, the meadows; nothing had changed. The clouds had vanished, the cows grazed peacefully in the evening sun. Beyond the horizon, Amsterdam, which he now knew better than Haarlem, but only in the way one knows someone else's face better than one's own.

He crossed to the sidewalk that had since been laid out along the embankment, walked on a bit, and only then jerked his face away from the water, in the other direction.

3

The three houses. An open space between the first and second, like a missing tooth. Only the fence was still there. It surrounded a thick vegetation of nettles and bushes with a few slender trees among them, like in some sixteenth-century paintings that have an angel on a hilltop and an ill-tempered crow staring at a monstrous moon. Many more weeds grew there than on the empty lots in back, perhaps because the ashes made it especially fertile. According to his uncle, in the hills of northern France there were places like this among the fields, places the farmers left unplowed because they were mass graves from the First World War.

In the shade, under the nettles, there were probably still some bricks, fragments of walls, foundations; and down in the earth, the cellar (his old scooter no doubt stolen out of it), everything filled with rubbish. Even though he had not thought about them, these ruins had been here all these years, without interruption.

Slowly, tilting his head a bit to the side, tossing his hair back now and then, he walked toward the spot where he had sat in the van, and once more looked at the empty space. While sparrows made a racket in the small trees, he saw the house rise up in front of him, built out of transparent bricks, the windowpanes and the thatch as he remembered them, the bay window and above it the little balcony of the bedroom, the pointed roof, and to the left, the dormer window of his room. On the board under the balcony were the letters

CAREFREE

The name of the Kortewegs' house had disappeared, painted over; but Hideaway and Bide-a-Wee were still there. He looked at the spot where Ploeg had been lying, ages ago. He saw him prone on the patterned bricks, as if drawn in contour with fluorescent chalk by the police. He was tempted to touch the spot, to lay his hands on it, and this worried him. Nevertheless, he did slowly cross the street—but before he reached the other side he saw something move at the window of Hideaway. Looking closely, he recognized Mrs. Beumer. She had already noticed him and waved.

He was upset. Not once had it occurred to him that she or any of the others might still be living here. That was inconceivable. He cared only about the place, not the people. Whenever he had thought about it, the Beumers, the Kortewegs, and the Aartses had not been present. That the people too had remained the same . . . he wanted to run away, but she was already standing in the doorway.

"Tonny!"

He could still have escaped. Probably it was his good manners that made him walk with a smile through the garden gate toward her.

"Hello, Mrs. Beumer!"

"Tonny, my boy." She took his hand and put her other arm around his waist, holding him with brief little squeezes against her, awkwardly, as if she had not embraced anyone in a long time. She had grown much older and smaller, her hair now completely white, with a tightly curled permanent. She would not let go of his hand. "Come in," she said, pulling him across the threshold. There were tears in her eyes.

"I'm afraid I really should . . ."

"Look who's here," she called through the door of the front parlor.

In an armchair dating from the previous century, which at that time had not become modern again but was still old-fashioned (the way it is now too, for the second time) sat Mr. Beumer, grown so old and thin that the crown of his head no longer reached the wood carving on the high-backed chair. His legs were hidden beneath a brown plaid blanket.

On top of it lay his hands, in continuous motion. His head constantly nodded. When Anton held out his hand, Mr. Beumer's came toward him like a wounded, fluttering bird. Anton held it but felt only the cool, feeble likeness of a hand.

"How are you doing, Hans?" he asked in a gentle, broken voice.

Anton looked at Mrs. Beumer. She made a gesture as if to say, this is the way things are.

"Fine, Mr. Beumer," he said. "Thank you. And how are you?"

But putting the question seemed to have exhausted Mr. Beumer. He nodded and said nothing more, continuing to observe Anton with small, watery blue eyes. The corners of his mouth were damp and shiny. The skin of his face was as thin as wax paper. Whatever hair he had left was straw-colored, the way Anton remembered it. Perhaps he had been a redhead long ago. A dark-brown radio made of Bakelite and shaped like an egg halved lengthwise was broadcasting a program for children. Mrs. Beumer had started clearing the table; apparently they had finished supper.

"Let me help you."

"No. Just make yourself comfortable and I'll fix you a cup of coffee."

He sat straddling the exotic stool by the fireplace, a camel saddle which had been familiar to him all his life. Mr. Beumer did not take his eyes off him. Anton smiled and looked about. Nothing had changed. At the dining room table stood the four black-lacquered chairs, with their intricately carved, pointed backs, rather gothic and creepy, that used to frighten him when he came here for tea and cake. Above the door still hung the crucifix with the twisted, yellowed Corpus. There was a sour smell in the room; all the windows were closed tight. So were the connecting doors with the leaded panes. "Weedywot," chanted the disguised woman's voice on the radio. "I see you but I pick you not." Suddenly

Mr. Beumer belched and looked about him in surprise, as if he heard something unexpected.

"Why didn't you come sooner, Tonny?" Mrs. Beumer called from the kitchen.

He got up and went to her. From the hall he could see that their bed stood in the back room, probably because Mr. Beumer could no longer climb the stairs. She poured a thin trickle of water over the coffee.

"This is the first time I've returned to Haarlem."

"He hasn't been well at all lately," Mrs. Beumer said softly. "Just pretend you don't notice."

Of course. What else? Should I burst out laughing and exclaim, "Don't talk nonsense!" But actually that would probably have been better, he realized.

"Obviously," he said.

"Do you know that you haven't changed at all? You're even taller than your father, but I recognized you at once. Are you still living in Amsterdam?"

"Yes, Mrs. Beumer."

"I knew that, because your uncle came right after the Liberation. My husband saw you being driven off in that German car, and we had no idea whether you were still alive. No one knew about anything in those dreadful times. You can't imagine how often we talked about you. Come."

They returned to the living room. When Mr. Beumer saw Anton he once more held out his hand, and Anton shook it in silence. Mrs. Beumer laid the Persian cloth, whose pattern he still remembered, back on the table. She poured the coffee.

"Do you take sugar and milk?"

"Just milk, please."

She poured some hot milk out of the small aluminum pan into the wide, low cup.

"To think that you should never have wanted to see this place again . . ." she said as she handed him the cup. "But actually I can understand it. It was just too awful, all that. Someone else has been here several times and stands looking at us from across the street."

"Who is it?"

"No idea. A man." She handed him the cookie tin. "A biscuit?"

"Please."

"Are you sure you're comfortable there? Why don't you sit at the table?"

"But this is my usual place." He laughed. "Don't you remember? When your husband read to me out of *The Three Musketeers*?"

Mrs. Beumer turned off the radio and sat sideways at the table. She laughed along with him, but a minute later her laughter died and her face turned red. Anton looked away. With thumb and finger he took the skin off his milk and lifted it slowly. It folded up like an umbrella, and he draped it over the edge of his saucer. He took a sip of the weak brew. Now something was expected of him, a question about long ago. His should be the opening move, no doubt, but he had no desire to begin. They probably thought that he was terribly disturbed by the past, dreamed about it every night, but the fact was that he almost never thought about it. As he sat before these two old people in this room, at least one of them must imagine him to be quite different from what he was. He looked at Mrs. Beumer. Once more there were tears in her eyes.

"Does Mr. Korteweg still live here?" he asked.

"He moved away a few weeks after the Liberation, no one knows where. He never came to say goodbye; neither did Karin. That was very odd. Right, Bert?"

It was as if she wanted to try once more to involve him in the conversation, and Mr. Beumer's nodding head seemed to be a sign of agreement, an assertive nodding that would not end till he died—how strange. He hadn't been offered any coffee, no doubt because the cup would be empty before it reached his mouth. She must be feeding him when there was no company.

"Nine years we were neighbors," said Mrs. Beumer. "We went through the whole War together, and then suddenly they disappear without a word. For days there was a pile of aquariums left standing on the doorstep, to be cleared out by the garbage collector."

"Those were terrariums," said Anton.

"Those glass things. Ach, he was a very unhappy man. He came by here a few times right after the death of his wife. Do you still remember Mrs. Korteweg?"

"Vaguely . . . not really."

"That was in about forty-two or forty-three. How old were you then?"

"Ten."

"There's a nice young couple with two children living there now."

Those terrariums. He remembered Korteweg as a big, surly man who would barely say hello to him. As soon as he came home, he would take off his jacket and roll up his shirt sleeves in a peculiar way—toward the inside, so that they looked like puffed sleeves gathered around his hairy arms. Afterwards he usually went upstairs to do something mysterious that aroused Anton's curiosity.

Karin often sat sunning herself in a deck chair, her dark-blond hair piled on top of her head and her skirt raised way above the knees, so that sometimes he even caught a glimpse of her underpants. She had pale-blue, somewhat protruding eyes and nicely shaped calves, which reminded him of the cross-section of a plane's wings as pictured in *Flyer's World*. At night when he lay thinking about her in bed, he often had an erection. He had no idea what to do about it, however, and would end by falling asleep. Whenever he crept through the hole in the hedge into the Korte-wegs' garden, Karin was willing to interrupt her sunning to play a board game with him. She was just a bit cross-eyed, which was very attractive.

One day, after she had sworn him to secrecy, she showed him her father's hobby. Upstairs in the back room, ten or fifteen terrariums with lizards in them stood about on small tables. Weirdly silent, their bodies S-shaped, their small hands holding onto tree bark, the creatures stared at him out of a past as deep and immovable as themselves. Though some of them seemed to be grinning broadly, their eyes spoke a different language, of a gravity so immovable and undisturbed as to be almost unbearable.

Anton set his teacup on the mantelpiece next to the clock. From the way Mrs. Beumer talked about Korteweg, he concluded that she had no idea what had happened with Ploeg's body. Apart from the Kortewegs themselves, he was probably the only one who knew. He had not even told his uncle and aunt, perhaps because the fewer the people who knew how absurd it all had been, the less absurd it would actually be.

"And next door?" he said.

"Mr. and Mrs. Aarts. They're still living there, but they've never even said hello to us. You never went there either—remember? They keep to themselves. The other day, too. Mr. Groeneveld wanted to get something done about all those weeds next door—"

"Groeneveld?"

"The family that's living at the Kortewegs' now. You must have noticed all the stuff that's growing where your house used to be."

"Yes," said Anton.

"All those seeds blow over to their place and into our garden; it's impossible to keep up with the weeding. He thought the community should do something about it. He wrote a letter, and we signed it, but Mr. Aarts pretended he wasn't home. Can you imagine? It wouldn't have been any trouble." She looked at him, offended.

Anton nodded. "It certainly is amazing, all those weeds."

From his tone Mrs. Beumer apparently got the impression that she had not been very tactful. Suddenly insecure, she said, "I mean . . ."

"I understand, Mrs. Beumer. Life continues."

"You're such an understanding boy, Tonny," she said happily. She stood up. "Another cup of coffee?"

"No thank you."

She poured herself some. "You remind me of that poor Peter," she said. "You don't look like him at all, but he was just as thoughtful. Always friendly, always helpful . . ." She let the lump of sugar, which she had been holding in the claws of the silver tongs, fall back into the sugar bowl. "You know . . . I thought his fate was the worst, somehow. That sweet boy. Your father and mother too, of course, but Peter . . . He was even younger than you are now. I thought it was so awful when I heard about it. I saw him try to help that man—Ploeg, I mean. After all, it wasn't certain that he was dead. Of course he was a scoundrel, I'm quite aware of that, but still he was human. A boy like Peter, with a heart of gold . . . it cost him his life."

Anton lowered his head and nodded. With his hands he caressed the brown leather of the stool made from the camel saddle. It too would have gone up in flames if Peter had had his way . . . If everything had happened according to Peter's plan, everything in this house would have been reduced to ashes. Mr. Beumer's armchair, Mrs. Beumer's kitchen, the crucifix, the macabre chairs around the dining table. In that case the troublesome weeds would have been growing on this spot, whereas his parents would still be living next door in Carefree. Mr. and Mrs. Beumer would probably have been too old to be shot, but what would have happened to Peter? He would have had to do his military service. In forty-seven during the police action in Indonesia, he would have been part of the Seventh of December Division. Maybe he would have set villages on fire; maybe he would have died there. Unimaginable, all that. Peter had never been more than seventeen years old, three years younger than Anton now, and that too was hard to imagine. He, Anton, was forever the younger brother, even if he should live to be eighty. It all was inconceivable.

Mrs. Beumer made the sign of the cross. "It's always the best ones," she said softly, "that God calls to him first."

Then Fake Ploeg was the best of us all, thought Anton.

"Yes," he said.

"God's ways are unfathomable. Why should he have been killed in front of your house? It might just as well have happened here, or at Mr. Korteweg's. We've often wondered about that, my husband and I. He always used to say that God had spared us, but how should we take that? Because that would mean that he didn't spare you, and why shouldn't he have spared you?"

"And then your husband answered," said Anton, feeling that perhaps he was going a bit too far, "that it was because we were heathens."

In silence Mrs. Beumer plucked at the tablecloth with the sugar tongs. For the third time tears welled in her eyes.

"That darling Peter . . . that sweet father and mother of yours. I still see him walk by here, your father, in his black coat, with his bowler hat and rolled-up umbrella. He always looked down at the ground. When he went out with your mother, he always walked one step ahead of her, the way the Indonesians do. They certainly never did anyone any harm . . ."

"Pickles are just like crocodiles," Mr. Beumer said suddenly.

His wife and Anton looked at him, but he stared back at them innocently.

Mrs. Beumer once more lowered her eyes to her hands.

"What they must have experienced! Surely your uncle told you about it. When your mother flew at that fellow . . . Simply slaughtered, like beasts."

It was as if an electric shock passed through Anton from his neck to his tailbone.

"Mrs. Beumer," he stammered. "Could you please . . ."

"Of course my boy, I understand. It was all so terrible."

He must leave at once. He looked at his watch without noticing what time it was.

"Goodness, I have to go. I hope you don't mind. I just came by for a second . . ."

"Of course, my boy." She stood up and smoothed the front of her dress with both hands.

"Is this really the first time that you've been back to Haarlem, Tonny?"

"Really."

"Then you should walk by the monument and have a look."

"Monument?" he said, surprised.

"There," said Mrs. Beumer and pointed to a corner of the room where on a small table stood a vase of tall, whitish plumes like peacock's feathers, or perhaps they were peacock's feathers. "On the place where it all happened."

"I never heard about it."

"How is it possible?" said Mrs. Beumer. "It was unveiled about three years ago by the burgomaster. Lots of people were invited. We had so hoped to see you then; my husband was still quite all right at the time. But I didn't see your uncle either. Shall I come along?"

"If you don't mind, I'd rather . . ."

"Of course," she said and took his hand in both of hers. "You, need to be alone with it. Goodbye, Tonny. It was so wonderful to see you again, and I'm sure it was for my husband too, even though he can't show it now."

Hand in hand they looked at Mr. Beumer. Exhausted, he had closed his eyes. She told Anton that his hands were just as large as his father's; then they took leave of each other. He promised he would return soon, but he knew that he would never see these people again. He would never come back to Haarlem.

As he stepped out of the front door, he was struck by the brightly lit open space to his left. Across from the wilderness he saw the new owners in the garden of the former Home at Last, a thin blond man with a little Indonesian wife, both about thirty-five. The man was playing soccer with a little boy as she looked on with a baby in her arms.

It was the lilac hour. The sun had just gone down, the quay and the meadows were bathed in a light that belonged neither to day nor night. It came out of another world where nothing ever moved or changed, and it lifted everything out of the ordinary. At the other end of the quay, where the road parted from the water, he saw a man-high hedge skirting the sidewalk that had not existed seven years ago. There was no traffic, and he crossed the road on a diagonal toward the monument.

The hedge, about a meter wide, was made of rhododendrons, whose leaves glistened in the magic light. It surrounded a low cement wall. On the square central base stood a grayish statue of a staring woman, hair hanging loose and arms reaching out. It was carved in a somber, symmetrically static, almost Egyptian style. Underneath was the date, with the words

THEY FELL
FOR QUEEN AND FATHERLAND

To left and right on two bronze plaques at the sides were the names of the dead in four rows. The last row read:

G. J. SORGDRAGER	b.	3.	6. 1919
W. L. STEENWIJK	b.	17.	9. 1896
D. STEENWIJK–van LIEMPT	b.	10.	5. 1904
J. TAKES	b.	21.	11. 1923
K. H. S. VEERMAN	b.	8.	2. 1921
A. van der ZON	b.	5.	5. 1920

Anton's eyes were riveted on the names. There they were, recorded and preserved in a bronze alphabet, the letters not even made of bronze, but in a bronze negative: the men who had jumped handcuffed out of the truck, his mother the only woman, his father the only one born in the last century. This was all that remained of them now. Except for a few photographs still preserved by his uncle and aunt, nothing was left but these names, and himself. Their graves had never been found.

Perhaps the provincial war monuments committee had debated whether their names really belonged here. Perhaps some of the officials had pointed out that the Steenwijks were, after all, not among the hostages, and were not really killed by a firing squad but simply murdered like animals. At which the officials of the central committee may also have questioned whether they deserved to be on the monument. At which, as a concession, perhaps the officials from the provincial committee had managed to obtain the exclusion of Peter. He belonged, at least in a broader sense, to those who had died as armed resistors, for whom there were other monuments. Hostages, members of the Underground, Jews, Gypsies, homosexuals—they shouldn't just be mixed up together, for God's sake; the end result would be a total mess.

The towpath was still there; the water was no longer frozen. When he saw that Mrs. Beumer still stood watching him behind the bay window, he did not return the way he had come.

Neither did he return to Van Lennep's party; he took the first train to Amsterdam. When he got home his aunt and uncle were still at the table, just finished with dinner. The lamp was lit. A bit put out, his uncle asked why he hadn't called to say he'd be late.

"I went to Haarlem," said Anton.

His uncle and aunt exchanged glances. The table was set for him and he sat down at his place. He picked up a piece of lettuce with his fingers, and tilting his head backwards, dropped it into his mouth.

"Shall I fry you an egg?" asked his aunt.

He shook his head, swallowed the lettuce, and asked his uncle, "Why didn't you ever tell me there's a monument standing on our quay?"

Van Liempt set down his cup of coffee, wiped his mouth, and looked him straight in the eye.

"I told you that, Anton."

"When did you?"

"Three years ago. It was unveiled in forty-nine. There was an invitation and I asked you if you wanted to go, but you didn't."

"I remember exactly what you said." Mrs. Van Liempt filled a plate with salad and put it in front of him. "You said they could go to hell with their monument, for all you cared."

"Don't you remember?" asked Van Liempt. Anton shook his head and kept silent. He looked at the white tablecloth and slowly drew four lines in it with his fork. For the first time he felt a kind of fear, something sucking him in, a deep hole into which things fell without reaching the bottom, as when someone throws a stone into a well and never hears it land.

At a time when he still thought about such things, he had wondered what would happen if he drilled a tunnel right through the center of the earth and then jumped in, wearing a fireproof suit. After a certain amount of time that could be determined mathematically, he would arrive, feet first, at the antipode, though he would not quite reach the surface.

He would come momentarily to a standstill. Then he would disappear once more, upside-down, into the depths. After many years, also mathematically calculable, he would at last stop and remain floating, weightless, at the center of the earth, where he would be able to reflect upon the state of things in eternity.

THIRD
EPISODE

1 9 5 6

1

Anton continued in medical school as a fair-to-middling student. A new stage in his life began in 1953, when, having passed his first exams, he left the house on the Apollolaan and rented an apartment in the center of town. In this small, dark place above a fish store, on a little street between the Prinsengracht and the Keizergracht, where only five or six meters separated him from his neighbors across the way, the Haarlem of 1945 sank even more into the background. The process of putting Haarlem behind him resembled the changes a man goes through when he divorces. He takes a girl friend to forget his wife, but just doing that prolongs the connection with the wife. Possibly things will work out only with the next girl friend—although the third one has the best chance. Boundaries have to be continuously sealed off, but it's a hopeless job, for everything touches everything else in this world. A beginning never disappears, not even with the ending.

Every few months or so he suffered from a daylong bout of migraine that forced him to lie down in the dark, though it hardly ever made him vomit. He read a lot, but never about the War, and once he published a few poems about nature in a student magazine, under the name of "Anton Peter." He played the piano (with a preference for Schumann) and enjoyed attending concerts. He had avoided going to the theater ever since, for incomprehensible reasons, he had felt indisposed during a splendid performance of Chekhov's *Cherry Orchard* directed by Charof. During a scene where a man sat at a table with bowed head while a woman outside on a terrace shouted at someone, Anton was overcome by a sense of something dreadful, something elusive but so overwhelming that he had to leave at once. Outside in the street, with the crowds, trolleys, and cars, his symptoms disappeared quickly and completely; a few minutes later he wondered if there had been anything to them.

Every week he went to the Apollolaan with a bag full of dirty laundry. Usually he stayed there for dinner, and as time went by he began to notice the extreme orderliness of this well-to-do middle-class life, the way everything was in its place, nothing ever broken, unpainted, improvised, or second-rate. Food was served in dishes, wine in decanters; jackets were never removed or ties loosened. Whenever his aunt or uncle happened to come to his apartment, he could tell by their faces that it gave them the opposite impression. Then his uncle would say that he too had been a student once.

In 1956 he passed his final exams and began to serve his internship in several hospitals. He had already decided to specialize in anesthesia. He knew that he could earn twice, even three times, as much if he became an internist or cardiologist with a private practice. But then he would have less time to himself and would probably develop an ulcer or heart disease, whereas an anesthesiologist could close the hospital doors behind him after an operation was finished. So could surgeons, of course, but surgery was only for butchers.

And there were not only negative reasons for his choice of anesthesiology. He was fascinated by the delicate equilibrium that must be maintained whenever the butchers planted their knives in someone—this balancing on the edge between life and death, and his responsibility for the poor human being, helpless in unconsciousness. He had, besides, the more or less mystical notion that the narcotics did not make the patient insensitive to pain so much as unable to express that pain, and that although drugs erased the memory of pain, the patient was nevertheless changed by it. When patients woke up, it always seemed evident that they had been suffering. But when he spoke of this theory once to his colleagues, who were talking about boat races, the way they looked at him suggested that he had better keep his thoughts to himself if he wanted to remain in the club.

And then there was politics. The talk went on forever, but he hardly bothered to follow it, especially on a national level. Though he read the headlines, he forgot them at once. When an English colleague questioned him about the Dutch system of government, Anton knew very little, no more than about the German or French. He bought newspapers mainly for the crossword puzzles; he couldn't resist them and had become an expert. Whenever he found an unsolved puzzle in a paper in some waiting room, it became his ambition to decipher the clue that had stymied the previous person. After he had filled all the blanks, he surveyed the completed square with satisfaction. The fact that most letters had a double function in both a horizontal and a vertical word, and that these words were paired in a mysterious way, pleased him no end. It had something to do with poetry.

But during that same year, 1956, the time came for him to vote in the elections. At his weekly dinner in the Apollolaan he asked his uncle which party he should endorse, though he said it would probably be the liberals. When his uncle asked why, Anton had no better reason than that his friends did. This was the worst possible reason, according to Van Liempt, who managed to change Anton's mind in a few minutes. Present-day liberalism, he said, combined a fundamental pessimism about social solidarity with the idea that the individual must remain as free as possible. But a person is either a pessimist who favors enforced order, or an optimist who favors freedom. It is impossible to be both at once. One cannot combine the pessimism of socialism with the optimism of anarchy, and yet this is what liberalism does. Therefore it is very simple, he said; you have only to decide whether you are an optimist or a pessimist. Which is it? Anton looked up at him briefly, lowered his eyes again, and said, "Pessimist."

And so he voted for the Social Democrats like his uncle, who was one of those important party leaders from whom burgomasters and ministers are chosen. Only later did Anton realize that almost nobody voted rationally, but simply out of self-interest, or because he felt an affinity for the members of a certain party, or because the leading candidate inspired confidence. It was physiobiological, in a way. In a subsequent election he voted somewhat more conservatively, for a newly founded party which claimed that the difference between right and left was obsolete. Still, national politics meant little to him: about as much as paper airplanes would mean to the survivor of a plane crash.

2

Later that year he became more aware of Communism, and at the same time of international politics. For the second half of 1956 provided a veritable orgy for newspaper readers: unrest in Poland, scandals within the royal family, the French and English attack on Egypt, the revolution in Hungary and the intervention of the Soviet Union, the landing of Fidel Castro in Cuba. A few weeks before this bravura performance in the Caribbean, the rumble of the Russian tanks which had rolled into Budapest still echoed within Holland, and nowhere more audibly than around the corner from Anton's apartment. There, in a large nineteenth-century building called Felix Meritis, were the headquarters of the Communist Party. Unruly mobs roamed the city, destroying everything that had anything to do with the Communists, from their bookstore to the windows of their homes. The crowds were aided by the press, which published addresses under the pretense of objective reporting. A paper would announce that the home of this or that Party leader on such-and-such a street had been only slightly damaged—and the next day the damage would be more extensive. After completing all this work, mobs of thousands gathered in front of the Felix Meritis building on the Keizergracht and besieged it continuously for forty-eight hours.

By then the building had become a fortress. Downstairs the windows were boarded up. None of the second-floor areas were still undamaged, and men in helmets were visible on the roof. Women too could be seen at times, and the crowds jeered at them with hostility. People who wanted to go in or out of the building made sure they had police protection. Policemen with rubber-tipped clubs and drawn guns tried to hold the crowd to the opposite side of the canal, but the police too were in danger from stones flying through the air. The men on the roof were throwing back the stones that had landed inside the building. Now and then they aimed fire hoses at small groups that came too close. A gray police boat patrolled the canal to fish out people who had fallen in the water.

Anton was totally uninterested in all this. He would never have taken part; he even avoided conversations about it. Somehow he couldn't help thinking that though it was all pretty terrible, it was only child's play, really. Besides, he got the impression that in a way, many people were delighted with what had happened in Budapest because it confirmed their opinions about Communism.

The worst problem for him was the constant racket. Since his own narrow street provided access to the back of the Felix Meritis building, on the Prinsengracht, demonstrators also gathered there and even threw Molotov cocktails, as the fishman told him. In desperation one evening he went to the movies, to see *The Seventh Seal*, and when he came home he put on loud music, Mahler's Second Symphony. But the noise didn't let up all night, and he decided to spend the following night in the Apollolaan, where everything was peaceful. When the time came, however, he couldn't believe that the uproar would go on for another night, so he went home as usual after work.

It was dusk, and candles were burning at many windows. The flag hung at half-mast from countless houses. He parked his scooter a few blocks away so it wouldn't be damaged by the mob, and walked to his little street.

The tumult had grown, if anything. He had trouble getting to his house through the crowd, and just as he reached the doorway, all hell broke loose. Police cars from the Keizergracht suddenly appeared and drove into the mob with blasting sirens and blazing lights, stepping on the gas, slamming on the brakes, then revving up again. Policemen on horseback with drawn swords now invaded the street, and motorcycles with sidecars rode up and down the sidewalks while helmeted policemen leaned out of them and hit people with the handles of long black poles. Panic broke out, but to his surprise Anton noticed that he, in contrast, became calmer. He had felt upset at first, yet now, with shouting and screaming everywhere, people being trampled, people bleeding and trying to reach safety, he was pervaded by a strange indifference. His doorway, which also led to the entrance of the fish store, was only about two meters square. Now a dozen people stood in it, crowding him against his front door. He already had his key in his hand but he realized that even if he could turn around, he mustn't open the door. If he did the staircase and his rooms would be invaded within minutes, and when the people left all his possessions would have disappeared.

In front of him stood a big fellow whose strong back was crushing Anton against the door with all its might, but of course it only seemed that way, for the man was being crushed himself. His hand gripped a big gray rock, which he had to hold up over his shoulder for lack of room. To protect his nose and in order not to suffocate, Anton turned his head to the side, but from the corner of his eye he saw the man's dirty nails and the calluses on his fingers.

Suddenly everyone ran out of the doorway. The man in front turned around briefly—perhaps to see who he had felt at his back all this time—stepped out into the street, turned around again, and stood still.

"Hello, Ton," he said.

Anton looked into the wide, coarse face. Suddenly he knew.

"Hello, Fake."

For a few seconds they eyed each other, Fake with the stone in his hand, Anton with the key. There was still movement on the street, but the center of the violence had shifted to the Prinsengracht.

"Come on up," said Anton.

Fake hesitated. He looked to right and left, as if reluctant to leave the excitement, but understood that he could not very well avoid it.

"Just for a minute, then."

When Anton heard the heavy footsteps following him on the stairs, he could hardly believe it was happening. He had never thought about Fake Ploeg again, yet Fake too had gone on existing and was still present in this world. They didn't shake hands. What were they supposed to talk about? Why in hell had he invited him in? He switched on the light and drew the curtains.

"You want a drink?"

To his horror, Fake put the stone on the grand piano Anton had been given for his birthday. He didn't slam it down, but Anton could hear that it had scratched the lacquer.

"A beer, if you've got it."

For himself, Anton poured a glass of wine out of the bottle left from last night. Ill at ease, Fake tried to get comfortable in the canvas chair that looked like a huge butterfly. Anton sat on the black couch with the worn-out springs.

"Cheers," he said, and wondered what to say next.

Fake briefly lifted his glass, then emptied half of it. Wiping his mouth with the back of his hand, he looked at the bookcase and the shelf with the sextants.

"Student, I suppose?"

Anton nodded. Fake nodded back. He shifted, straightened, and tried to get more comfortable.

"No good?"

"What a lousy chair," said Fake.

"It's the latest fashion, you know. Come on, sit here." They changed places. Fake stared at him as if he could see him better now.

"Do you know you haven't changed at all?"

"So I'm told."

"I recognized you right away."

"It took me a moment," said Anton. "I didn't see your father that often."

Fake pulled a pack of tobacco out of his inside pocket and began to roll a cigarette. When Anton offered him a pack of Yellow Dry, he declined. Maybe Anton shouldn't have said it, but it was true: Fake was the image of his father, only younger and thinner and a bit puffier. Besides, he didn't think it was up to him to be careful of Fake's feelings. He wished the telephone would ring, so he could say to whoever it was that he would come to the hospital at once. It was cold and damp in the room.

"I'll light the stove," he said.

He got up and opened the kerosene valve. Fake rolled his cigarette, picked the extra tobacco out of both ends, and stuffed it back into the package, which he held daintily between his ring and little finger.

"What are you studying?"

"Medicine."

"I work for a household appliance store," said Fake before Anton got a chance to ask him. "Repairs, you know."

Anton waited till enough oil had dripped into the stove.

"In Haarlem?"

Fake looked at him as if he were crazy. "Did you really think we could go on living in Haarlem?"

"How should I know?"

"Can't you imagine that we had to get out of there in a hurry, after the War?"

"Yes, I guess so," said Anton. He lifted the lid off the stove and dropped the burning match into it. "Where are you living now?"

"In Den Helder."

The match went out and he lit a second one. He dropped it and faced his visitor.

"Did you come to Amsterdam just to throw stones?"

"Yes," said Fake and looked at him. "Strange, isn't it?"

Anton put the lid back on the stove and sat down. If he simply suggested that they put an end to this meeting, Fake would probably get up and go at once. But suddenly he felt stubborn, as if he didn't want Fake to think that he could get rid of him that easily.

"Is your mother still alive?"

Fake nodded. "Yes," he said after a silence. He made it sound like a kind of admission, as if Anton had asked, is *your* mother still alive? He hadn't meant it that way—but even as he said it he realized that perhaps it was what he had meant, after all.

"How come you're working in one of those appliance stores?" he asked. "You went to high school, after all."

"Only one semester."

"Why didn't you stay on?"

"Do you really care?" asked Fake, poking a bit of tobacco back into his cigarette with the end of his match.

"Why would I ask if I didn't?"

"After the War they arrested my mother and put her in a camp. I ended up in a Catholic boarding school, which was connected to the Episcopal industrial school. So I had to go there, even though I wasn't a Catholic."

"What was your mother accused of?"

"Ask the gentlemen of the Special Judiciary. They probably suspected her of being married to my father." From his tone Anton could tell that Fake had said this before, and it didn't sound as if he had thought it up himself, either.

"And then?"

"After nine months they let her go, but by that time other people were living in our house. We were offered a place in Den Helder where nobody knew us. So I went to trade school there."

"And why didn't you go back to high school?"

"You really don't understand anything, do you?" Fake screwed up his face as if he smelled something rotten. "What do you think? My mother had to become a cleaning woman to support me and my sisters. You know—one of those women with a rag around their heads and a shopping bag, like you see on the streets at six-thirty in the morning. The bag was to carry her brushes and mops and soaps. She had to buy those herself. When she came home at night, she walked slower and slower. And now she's in the hospital, if you really want to know, with water running out of her right leg. That one is all yellow with brown spots. The left leg was amputated two weeks ago. Now are you satisfied, Doctor?" He emptied his glass, slammed it down on the table, and leaned back. "So that's the difference, right? We're in the same class, your parents are shot, but you're doing medical studies all the same, whereas my father was shot and I repair water heaters."

"But your mother is alive," said Anton promptly, "and your sisters too." Now he weighed his words carefully. They were on dangerous ground. "Besides, isn't there some difference between your father's and my parents' deaths?"

"What difference?" Fake asked aggressively.

"My parents were innocent."

"My father too," he said without a moment's hesitation, his eyes on Anton. Anton, amazed, kept silent. Perhaps Fake actually meant it. Perhaps he was really convinced of it.

"All right," Anton said, at last, with a conciliatory gesture. "All right. I only know what I heard, but . . ."

"Exactly."

". . . but if it really is your opinion that social injustice caused this difference between us, then I don't understand that stone." With his head he motioned to the ugly stone that was still lying like an insult on his grand piano. "Then you should have been a Communist instead."

Before Fake answered, he took his glass and poured the last drops down his throat. "Communism," he said calmly, "is the worst. Just look at Budapest, where an entire people's drive for freedom is being drowned in blood."

"Fake," said Anton, irritated, "I'm no Communist either, but that doesn't mean I find it necessary to learn those headlines by heart."

"Sure, of course Doctor Steenwijk is clever enough to say it better in his own words. Excuse me if I'm not that smart. People are killing each other over there. Is that any better? What do you suppose the political commissars are doing over there? There's mass murder going on over there, didn't you know? Did you read *Het Parool*? About the atrocities being committed by Mongol soldiers?"

"Mongol soldiers!" Anton said. "What do you mean, Fake? Has the time come now to send Mongols to the gas chamber?"

"No, you bastard!" said Fake with a threatening look. "I'm not sure what you're getting at, but I can tell you one thing: at least my father was absolutely right about the Communists. He used to predict everything that's going on now. It's no coincidence that it was the same damned Communists who killed him. The same bunch that you see now running over the rooftops with helmets on their lousy heads. Why are you defending them anyway? Remember, they knew very well that there would be reprisals, yet they shot him down in front of your house. They couldn't have cared less, otherwise they'd have taken the trouble to hide the body. Besides, it didn't end the War one second sooner."

He stood up and took his glass over to the table where Anton had left the open beer bottle. Anton noticed that the stove still wasn't burning. He too stood up, tore a strip from a newspaper, lit it, and dropped it onto the black, shiny layer of oil.

He poured himself another glass of wine. And because Fake remained standing, Anton did too. Outside there was more shouting and the sound of sirens.

"My family," Anton said, massaging his neck with his empty hand, "was not executed by the Communists but by your father's friends."

"But those Communists knew what would happen."

"Therefore they were to blame?"

"Right. Who else?"

"Fake," said Anton. "I understand that you'd want to defend your father. He was, after all, your father. But if your father had been my father, if everything had been turned around, would you then be defending Fake Ploeg? Let's not kid each other. Your father was killed by the Communists with premeditation because they had decided that it was essential, but my family was senselessly slaughtered by Fascists, of whom your father was one. Isn't that right?"

Fake turned his back to Anton and remained motionless, bent slightly forward, as he asked, "Are you implying it was my father's fault that your family was murdered?"

Now, Anton realized, every word mattered. Above the mantelpiece hung a tall mirror with an intricately carved frame, bought for a song at the flea market to make his room look bigger. In the weathered glass he saw that Fake had closed his eyes.

"Why can't you love your father without trying to whitewash him?" asked Anton. "After all, it doesn't take much to love a saint. That's like loving animals. Why don't you simply say: my father was definitely a collaborator, but he was my father and I love him."

"But dammit, he was not a collaborator, at least, not in the way you're implying."

"But suppose you knew for certain," Anton said to his back, "that he had done terrible things . . . God knows . . . just name something . . . wouldn't you still love him?"

Fake turned around, looked at him briefly, and began to pace up and down through the room. "Collaborator . . . collaborating . . ." he said after a while. "That's what they call it, and yet now they all think the way he did about Communism. Listen to what's going on out there. What's the difference between that and the Eastern Front? And all that stuff about the Jews; he didn't know a thing about that. He was ignorant of all that. You can't blame him for it, what the Germans did to them. He was with the police and simply did his duty, what he was told. Even before the War he had to arrest people, and he didn't know what would happen to them then, either. Of course he was a Fascist, but a good one, out of conviction. Things would have to change in Holland; it shouldn't ever go back to the way it was under Minister Colijn, when my father had to fire on workers. At least he didn't just follow the crowd, like most Hollanders. If Hitler had won the War, how many people in Holland would still be against him now, do you suppose? Don't make me laugh, man. Not till they saw that Hitler was losing did they all suddenly join the Resistance, those yellow bastards."

The stove, in which he had put too much oil, began to sputter in dull, rhythmic spurts. Fake gave it a professional glance and said, "That's never going to work." But he would not be distracted. With his glass in both hands he sat down on the window seat and asked, "Do you know when my father became a member of the National Socialist Party? In September, nineteen forty-four, after Mad Tuesday, when the whole thing was as good as lost and all those phony Fascists fled to Germany, or suddenly decided to join the

Resistance. That's when he thought it was time to take a stand. My mother often told us this. And because of his conviction they shot him—for nothing else—and that's what cost your family their lives. If the Communists hadn't done that, your father and mother would be here today. Possibly my father would have spent a couple of years in prison, and by now he would be back simply working for the police."

He straightened up and walked to the piano, on which he played a few notes in the middle register. The sound, mixed with the sputtering of the stove, reminded Anton of Stravinsky. Each word of Fake's made his head ache worse. How could anyone embroil himself in such a web of lies? Love was what caused it all—love, through thick and thin.

"To hear you tell it," he said, "your father's name belongs on that monument too."

"What monument?"

"The one back there on our quay."

"Is there a monument?"

"I didn't find out till much later myself. It has my parents' names and those of the twenty-nine hostages. Should Fake Ploeg be on it too?"

Fake looked at him and wanted to say something, then suddenly began to sob. The sobs rose out of him as if they belonged to someone else who was inhabiting his body.

"Shit . . ." he said, but it was unclear whether he was replying to Anton's question or angry with himself for crying. "As your house went up in flames, we got the news that our father was dead. Did you ever think of that? I've thought of what you went through; did you ever do the same for me?"

He turned toward him, then away, passed his hand over his eyes in despair, and suddenly grabbed the stone. He looked about, looked at Anton, who raised his arms to his head in self-defense and cried, "Fake!"

Fake took aim and threw it straight at the mirror. Anton ducked. With averted face he saw the glass break into large pieces that landed in splinters on the iron lid of the stove, which was now sputtering feebly. The stone bounced onto the mantelpiece and remained lying there. Surveying the damage with pounding heart, he heard Fake's footsteps run down the stairs.

A final fragment slipped out of the frame and shattered into pieces. Immediately afterwards the lid of the stove blew off with a dull thud, five centimeters up in the air, and let out a cloud of soot. Anton crossed his hands behind his neck, cracked his fingers, and took a deep breath. He felt on the verge of hysterical laughter. The shattered mirror, the exploding stove, the screaming in the street—with his headache he couldn't stand it. How senseless, all this! The soot spread through the room, and he knew it would take hours to clean it up.

He heard Fake come back up the stairs; only then did he realize that the street door had never closed.

"I wanted to tell you," Fake said, "that I'll never forget that time in the classroom."

"What time in the classroom?"

"That time you came in, when I was sitting there in my monkey suit."

"Oh God, yes," said Anton. "That happened too."

Fake hesitated. Perhaps he wanted to shake hands, but he just raised one briefly and went downstairs again. A minute later the door slammed in its lock.

Anton looked about. All his things were covered with a veil of grease. The books and the sextants were the worst. Fortunately the piano had been closed. First he had to clean up, headache or no headache. He drew the curtains and opened the windows wide. As the noise invaded the room, he looked at the shards. On the reverse side they were a dull black. Only a few sharp splinters were still stuck in the frame, which encircled nothing but dark brown wood that had once been papered over with newspapers, now mostly torn off. The two gilt putti, with their fruit platter and tails made of curled leaves, looked down at him with unchanged angelic expressions.

First he must get rid of the stone. He might simply throw it out of the window. Carefully, so as not to slip on the glass lying on the straw carpet, he went to the mantelpiece. Holding the stone in his hand, he read a fragment on a strip of newspaper still sticking to the wooden back of the mirror: NEL DI 2 LUGLIO 1854. SOLENNIZZANDOSI CON SACRA DEVOTA POMPA NELL'AUGUSTO TEMPIO DI MARIA SS. DEL SOCCORSO. "On the second of July, 1854. Celebrated with sacred ceremony at the Church of Blessed Mary of Perpetual Help."

One more thing he would never have found out if it hadn't been for Fake.

FOURTH
EPISODE

1 9 6 6

1

In love, too, he simply let things happen to him. Every few weeks a different girl would come and sit on his worn-out couch, usually with her legs folded under her, and he would explain the mechanism of a sextant one more time. This never bored him; he was fascinated by the shiny brass instruments with their small mirrors, measured scales, and little telescopes containing the night sky and the stars. Often the girls couldn't understand the apparatus, but always they understood the absorption with which he explained, and which therefore was directed a little at them. At times the couch remained empty for a week or two, which didn't bother him much. It was not his style to go to a bar to pick someone up.

In 1959 he passed his final medical exams and, having become an assistant anesthesiologist, rented a larger apartment with lots of light in the neighborhood of the Leidseplein. Every morning he walked the few blocks to the Wilhelmina Hospital, which had been called the Western Hospital during the War. In the streets around the complex of buildings, there was always much coming and going of ambulances, visitors, and patients taking a first stroll, wearing striped pajamas under their overcoats. Doctors walked from one building to another, their white coats casually unbuttoned. Anton, his head slightly to one side, tossing back his hair now and then, somewhat careless in manner, aroused the motherly instinct in the nurses bicycling by, who would then end up on his couch. Sometimes he had to pass the shed on which Lazarett had been written, but this reminded him less and less of Schulz, who had been brought here dying, or already dead.

He met his first wife in London in 1960, when he was there on Christmas vacation. During the day he strolled about the city, bought clothes on Regent Street, and dropped in on the dealers in antique navigational instruments behind the British Museum. At night he usually went to a concert. Most men still wore bowlers and carried rolled-up umbrellas. When he lunched in a pub, the umbrella stand would be full of those endearing instruments. One rainy afternoon, strolling down Whitehall between its colossal monuments to power, where the Horse Guard performed its inexplicable dances like strutting roosters, he decided to enter Westminster Abbey for the first time.

It was full of foreign tourists and day trippers from the country. He had bought a guidebook bound in the kind of purplish red common throughout England. For the central nave just at the entrance to the choir, it listed the one hundred and seventy graves of the finest flower of the nation, dating from the last six centuries. He closed the book. Everywhere, on the pavement, in the walls, and on the pillars, were sculptures and inscriptions. In the chapels, statues and tombstones stood just as if they were on display at a secondhand furniture auction. In the narrow passage along the choir the dead were aligned end to end, the way patients sometimes lay on stretchers in the hall in front of the operating rooms; only here, on their backs, in marble, on top of their sarcophagi, they were permanently anesthetized. He tried to imagine what would happen on Judgment Day, when they would all rise from their tombs and be introduced to each other, these hundreds of heroes, noblemen, and artists, the most exclusive club in the United Kingdom.

Royalty lay in the chapel behind the main altar. Past the throng of kings and queens shuffled the people who would never be buried here. At the Coronation Chair they came to a standstill. He himself was fascinated by this throne on which every ruler had been crowned since the fourteenth century. Ancient oak, simply ornamented, the back scratched full of initials from one century or another. In the true spirit of historical veracity, it had never been cleaned up. Under the wooden seat, a large stone: the Stone of Scone. Anton opened his guidebook again. The stone had once been the pillow of the biblical Jacob. It had ended up in Ireland (via Egypt and Spain) during the eighth century before Christ, then fourteen hundred years later in Scotland, and finally in England, where it could be seen at this very moment and on this spot. Just as the real truth about the kings all around him could be found only in Shakespeare's plays, so also this legend about the stone seemed to reveal an essential truth. Only if the Irish claimant to the throne had royal blood would the stone groan at coronation time; otherwise not. Anton burst out laughing and said aloud, "How true!" Upon which a young woman next to him asked, "What's true?"

He looked at her, and at that moment everything was decided.

It was her glance, the look in her eyes, and her hair, thick, springy, reddish hair. Her name was Saskia De Graaff, and she was a stewardess with KLM. After having visited the Poet's Corner as well, they went off together. She had to pick her father up at a club in St. James's. Every year he went to London for Christmas to meet his old wartime friends. As they arrived at the club building and made plans to meet in Amsterdam, they saw a general come down the stairs and step into a waiting car with a military driver.

A week later, during their first meeting in the lobby of the Hotel Des Indes, De Graaff inquired tactfully about his family. Anton said that his father had been a clerk at the law courts in Haarlem, but that both his parents had died long ago. Not till six months later, one warm evening in Athens, where De Graaff was ambassador, did he tell the whole story to his future father-in-law. Having heard him out, De Graaff remained silent and gazed from the darkened room into the brilliant, perfumed garden, vibrant with the chirping of crickets, where a small fountain murmured as it spouted up into the air. A servant in a white jacket clinked some pieces of ice together on the terrace. Saskia and her mother were sitting out there. The Acropolis could be seen in the distance between cypresses and pine trees. All De Graaff said after a while was, "Even the good has its evil side in this world. But there is still another side."

He himself had belonged to an organization that coordinated all the Resistance groups, and as such had been in direct contact with the exiled government in London. He too spoke little of those days. All Anton knew about them was what Saskia had told him, but he had no desire to hear more. He could probably have read up on the subject in the reports from the Parliamentary Inquest Committee, but he didn't.

A year after their first meeting, they got married. His uncle was not there; a senseless auto accident had put an end to his life. Shortly after his wedding Anton got a permanent job, and with financial help from De Graaff they bought half of a two-family house in the neighborhood behind the Concertgebouw.

2

During the heat wave at the beginning of June, 1966, Saskia had to attend the funeral of one of her father's friends, an important journalist and poet by the name of Sjoerd, whom she too had known after the War. She asked Anton to come with her, and he had managed to get the day off. He wanted to take their four-year-old, Sandra, along as well.

"Should we, Ton?" asked Saskia. "Death isn't exactly for children."

"I've never heard such a ridiculous platitude," he said. It sounded sharper than he intended. He excused himself and kissed her. They decided to go to the beach after the funeral.

His father-in-law, who was as old as the century, had retired and was living in a country house in Gelderland. He would be coming by car. Saskia called and suggested that he pick them up—then they could have coffee together first. A typical country dweller, he replied that he wouldn't be caught dead in Amsterdam; what did they think, that he wanted to be attacked by a gang of hippie Provos? He laughed as he said it, but he didn't come, though God knows he'd faced worse dangers in his life.

The funeral was in a village north of Amsterdam. The Steenwijks parked their car on the outskirts and walked to the small church, the two adults perspiring in their dark clothes, while Sandra, dressed in white, didn't mind the sun. In the village square was a crowd of men and women, mostly older, who all seemed to be acquainted. They greeted each other, not somberly and mournfully, but with laughter and exuberant embraces. There were many photographers. A cabinet minister—the one who had recently been much in the news in connection with the Amsterdam riots—stepped out of a big black Cadillac. He too was greeted with kisses and slaps on the back.

"These people all fought against the Germans," Anton told his daughter.

"In the War," she said as if she knew all about it, and twisted her doll's head with a decisive gesture.

Anton surveyed the scene with a continuous feeling of excitement. He knew no one. Saskia greeted a few people, though she had forgotten their names. Inside the bare Protestant church, where the organ was already playing, they sat in the last row. When the coffin was carried in, everyone stood up. He put his arm around Sandra, who asked in a whisper whether that gentleman was inside there now. On De Graaff's arm the widow entered—sad, of course, but facing the people with head high, nodding now and then with a gentle smile.

Suddenly Sandra called out, "Grandpa!"

He turned to her briefly and winked. They sat down in front, near the cabinet minister.

Anton recognized the mayor of Amsterdam. The funeral address was given by a famous clergyman who had spent years in a concentration camp. His delivery was so melodramatic that he seemed to have acquired his rhetorical manner by overcoming a speech defect, like Demosthenes training with the pebbles in his mouth. He made Sandra look up and wink with amusement at her father. Anton, only half listening, was struck by the profile of a woman across the aisle and a few rows ahead. For some reason it made him think of a sword, with its sharp tip planted straight in the ground. She must have been about forty-five; her dark hair, thick and bushy, was graying in places.

They joined the rear of the procession to the cemetery behind the church. During the short walk on the street and then along the gravel paths, everyone was again deep in conversation. There were many comings and goings, some people walking ahead, others falling back to the rear. It was not so much a funeral as a reunion.

"They feel at home again," said Saskia.

"I hope no one finds out that they're all here in one place."

"What do you mean, no one?"

"The Germans, of course."

"Don't be silly." Photographers were once more tracking down celebrities; the villagers stood looking on from across the street. All these years most of them had probably been unaware of the important personage living in their midst . . . Boys on motorbikes observed the procession with mocking faces, but their motors were silent. Obviously something about these men and women, a few of them disabled, impressed the boys enough to behave themselves.

"Papa?"

"Yes?"

"What is war, really?"

"A big quarrel. Two bunches of people who want to chop each other's heads off."

"You don't have to overdo it," said Saskia.

"You think so?" Anton laughed. At the cemetery a tight circle had formed around the grave, and the Steenwijks couldn't see much. Sandra got bored, so Saskia took her hand and led her on a walk. Behind him he could hear her reading inscriptions on the graves and explaining them. Now and then, ignoring the fact that his clothes were sticking to him, he lifted his face to the bright sun. The soft murmur in the last rows of the crowd did not die down until the widow herself addressed them, but her words were lost to him in the wide-open space of this sunny day. The birds flying overhead must have seen the people gathered here in the open landscape of the polders, around the small, dark hole in the earth that was like a big eye looking up at heaven.

The Steenwijks finally managed to offer their condolences to the widow at the end of the reception line in the parish house. Then, between cars starting up, they crossed over to the café on the other side of the street. The few outside tables were already taken by the villagers, and inside too it was busy. A crowd was gathering at the bar, tables were being pushed together, ties loosened, jackets removed, and loud calls issued for beer, coffee, and sandwiches. The jukebox was playing "Strangers in the Night." The cabinet minister was there talking to the burgomaster and scribbling something on the back of a cigarette box. Famous writers were present, as well as a notorious Provo. Just as Saskia suggested that they go somewhere else, her father came in. He sat down at a large table in the back, probably reserved, with about seven other men, some of whose faces were familiar to Anton. Evidently his wife had gone back to the house with the widow and the family. When he saw his daughter and Anton, he beckoned to them.

At the table he was in his element. In no time three conversations were going. In the one that he joined, he was on the defensive without losing his good humor, evidently quite aware that he was in control. A man with a blond forelock and still blonder eyebrows leaned toward him and said that he was becoming a real old bore. How in heaven's name could he compare the Vietnamese Liberation Front to the Nazis? The trouble was that he thought Americans were still the same as in World War Two. But actually it was the Americans who had changed and who should now be compared to the Nazis.

De Graaff leaned back with a laugh, holding onto the edge of the table with outsretched arms so that the men on his right and left also had to lean backwards. With his thinning white hair and imposing features he looked like the leader at a gathering of commissars, or the chairman presiding at a board meeting. "Jaap, my dear fellow," he began condescendingly, but the blond man interrupted him at once.

"Oh, I know; next you'll say I must have forgotten that the Americans came to our rescue."

"That's not at all what I was going to say."

"I'm not so sure. In any case I haven't forgotten a thing, but you did forget something."

"And what's that, may I ask?"

"The Russians also came to our rescue, even though we didn't see them here in our streets. They're the ones who defeated the German army, and it's still the Russians who are on the right side in Vietnam."

The man with the black mustache who sat behind De Graaff's left arm said icily, "How about leaving this kind of talk to other people?"

"But it's the truth," said Jaap. "The Russians have been de-Stalinized, but the Americans have become mass murderers." The man on the left shrugged and smiled politely under his mustache, suggesting that though he agreed, he felt that Jaap had started a pointless quarrel.

"Dirty Commies, all of them," said De Graaff good-naturedly in Anton's direction. "First-class fellows."

Anton smiled back. Obviously this conversation was a kind of game that they had played many times before.

"Sure, sure," said Jaap. "First-class fellows. But from nineteen forty-four on, Gerrit, you and your military government were no longer so much against the Germans as against the first-class fellows." Anton's father-in-law was not named Gerrit but Godfried Leopold Jérôme; in this company they apparently still addressed each other with their Underground pseudonyms. Jaap too was obviously not named Jaap.

"Well, what do you expect? The Krauts had been defeated, after all." Innocently De Graaff looked at Jaap. "Were we supposed to exchange one tyranny for another?" Gradually his smile faded.

"Go to hell," said Jaap.

"You ought to be grateful to us. If you'd had your way in 1945, you wouldn't have been expelled from the Party, as you are now; you'd have faced the firing squad. Certainly in your ambiguous position you wouldn't have had a chance with the Stalinists. No more than Slansky, in Czechoslovakia. I was posted in Prague at the time of his execution. You owe your life to the military government." And since Jaap didn't answer: "Always better to be at the head of the soccer club on the dung heap of history, than dead. Right?"

The large man on De Graaff's other side, a well-known poet with a satanic expression in his slanted eyes, crossed his arms and began to laugh.

"I have a feeling this is going to be an interesting conversation," he said.

"Sure," said Jaap. "Let him win his argument, for all I care."

"Do you know these verses of Sjoerd's?" asked De Graaff, and raising his finger, he declaimed:

When to the will of tyrants
A nation's head is bowed,
It loses more than life and goods—
Its very light goes out.

"Amazing, the uses of poetry—to justify the bombing of villages with napalm," said the man with the mustache. "But of course, that's only in Asia. Besides, during the Indonesian troubles you were already playing a peculiar role. 'Indies lost, heavy the cost,' and other such nonsense. Not a very good rhyme, if you ask me, but ask our expert here about that."

"An insignificant rhyme," said the poet.

"There you have it. Those very Indonesian police actions cost our deceased friend Sjoerd a few years of his life. And yet we've never had it so good in Holland as since we got rid of the Indonesian colonies."

"Thanks to the help of the Marshall Plan, dear Henk," said De Graaff sweetly. "Financed by the Americans, remember?"

"They owed it to us, we don't have to thank them for it. The American Revolution was financed by banks in Amsterdam. That one happened to be the revolt of an English colony, dear Gerrit. We're paying back the Marshall Plan to the last penny, whereas I'm not at all sure we got back a cent of that money in the eighteenth century."

"Must look it up," said De Graaff.

"And I'm no Communist, by the way. I'm an anti-Fascist. But because Communism is the greatest enemy of Fascism, I happen to be anti-anti-Communist, that's for certain."

"Do you know why De Graaff happened to be in the Resistance?" Jaap asked suddenly. "Do you know *who* he did it for? For the *little princesses* . . ." His tone implied that he wanted to vomit.

"Absolutely," said De Graaff, once more with a satisfied grin.

106

"An ordinary House of Orange Fascist, that's what you are, nothing else."

"I'm getting out of here," said Saskia, and stood up. "I don't need this. See you later!"

While De Graaff exclaimed, "An honorary title, an honorary title!" Anton stood up. The crowd parted to give him a brief glimpse of the woman he had been staring at in church. In the meantime his father-in-law was laughing loudly, obviously in his element.

"What do you know about the secret charms of the monarchy?" he cried with mock arrogance. "What is more beautiful and uplifting to the soul than the Palace of Soestdijk by night? All the windows lit, black limousines driving in and out, orders ringing out over the lawns, gentlemen wearing gala uniform with shiny swords, ladies in evening dress with glistening jewels walking up the steps to the front terrace, being greeted by handsome young officers in the marines. Inside, the glitter of chandeliers, lackeys with large silver trays full of glasses of champagne, and perhaps even a glimpse of a member of the royal family; if God be willing, perhaps even Her Majesty the Queen. And far away, in the drizzling rain, behind the gates guarded by military police, the grim populace . . ."

"I actually think you mean it, by God," said the poet who had predicted that this would be an interesting conversation. "Jesus Christ, if I were as much of a bastard as you, I wouldn't ever get a single word printed again." Some spit flew out of his mouth and ended up on De Graaff's dark-blue lapel, not far from the decoration in his buttonhole.

"Which, according to some of our more distinguished scholars, would be a blessing for our nation's literature," said De Graaff.

"Don't let it get you, man!" said Henk to the furious poet.

De Graaff pulled out his handkerchief and wiped away the white spit bubble. The knot of his gray tie was perfectly centered and disappeared with an elegant curve inside his vest. Jaap too had to laugh. The man sitting on the other side of the poet, a prominent publisher, rubbed his hands and exulted:

"A fierce afternoon!"

"The grim populace," said Henk, "has recently been bombarding your beloved royal family with stink bombs."

"*Stink* bombs . . ." said De Graaff with mock contempt.

"And that will cost you your head," Henk continued to someone standing behind Anton.

Anton turned around. He realized that the heat he had felt on his neck all this time came from the powerful Calvinist rump of the clergyman. The latter had apparently been following the conversation.

"Possibly," he said.

"And then?"

"Then I'll have another drink." He lifted his glass of Dutch gin, exchanged a glance of complicity with De Graaff, and turned away.

Suddenly silence fell at the table. Only the two men sitting on Anton's left were still involved in a subdued private conversation that they had been carrying on all the time.

Anton caught the following sentence: "I shot him first in the back, then in the shoulder, and then in the stomach as I bicycled past him."

3

Far away, deep inside the tunnel of the past, Anton heard the six shots ring: first one, then two, then two more, and finally one last shot. His mother looks at his father, his father at the sliding doors, Peter lifts the lid of the carbon lamp . . .

Anton turned to the man he had been sitting next to all this time. Before he knew what he was doing, he had already asked: "Wasn't there a fourth and a fifth shot? And then one more, a sixth?"

The other looked at him with half-closed eyes. "How do you know?"

"Are you talking about Ploeg, Fake Ploeg in Haarlem?"

A few seconds went by before the other man asked slowly, "Who are you? How old are you?"

"I was living there. It happened in front of our house. At least . . ."

"In front of your . . ." The man caught his breath. He had understood at once. Only on the operating table had Anton seen anyone lose all color so rapidly. The man had had the swollen, blotchy-red complexion of someone who drinks too much. As if the light had changed, he now turned as pale and waxen as old ivory. Anton began to tremble.

"Oh oh!" said the man two chairs away. "Now you're in trouble."

Everyone at the table noticed at once that something was wrong. The silence deepened; then confusion set in, with everyone talking at once, some standing up. De Graaff wanted to come between them, explaining that Anton was his son-in-law, but the man insisted on handling it himself. Then, to Anton, as if he wanted to fight it out, "Come outside."

He took his jacket from the back of his chair, grabbed Anton by the hand, and pulled him along through the crowd as if he had been a child. And that's how it felt to Anton, the hot hand of that man twenty years his senior, dragging him along—something he had never felt with his uncle, only sometimes with his father. In the other part of the café no one was aware of what was going on. Laughing, they let the two pass. "It's been a hard day's night . . ." the Beatles were singing on the jukebox.

Outside, he was struck by the silence. The village square lay shimmering in the sun. Here and there groups of people

were still standing about, but Saskia and Sandra were nowhere in sight. "Come," said the man, having surveyed the
scene. They crossed to the cemetery and entered through
the wrought-iron gate. Villagers had gathered around the
open grave to read the inscriptions on the ribbons and cards
that accompanied the flowers. Chickens from a neighboring
farm walked about the paths and the other graves. Near a
stone bench in the shade of an oak tree the man stood still
and held out his hand.

"Cor Takes," he said. "And your name is Steenwijk."

"Anton Steenwijk."

"They call me Gijs," he said, tossing his head in the direction of the café, and sat down.

Anton sat next to him. He didn't need any of this. He had
said what he did in spite of himself, as a reflex, the way a
nerve reacts to the impulse of a tendon. Takes produced a
pack of cigarettes, pulled one halfway out, and offered it to
him. Anton shook his head and faced him. "Listen," he said.
"Let's get up and walk out of here and never mention it
again. There's nothing to discuss, really. What happened,
happened. It doesn't bother me, believe me. It happened
over twenty years ago. I have a wife and child and a good
job. Everything is fine. I should have kept my mouth shut."

Takes lit a cigarette, inhaled deeply, and gave him a grim
look. "But you didn't keep your mouth shut." And after a
pause, "So now it happened." Only at the second sentence
did the smoke accompany his words.

Anton nodded. "Right," he said. He couldn't evade the
somber, dark-brown eyes staring at him. The left one was
different from the right, the eyelid somewhat heavier, its
piercing glance leaving him defenseless. Takes must have
been about fifty, but his lank, darkish-blond hair was graying only slightly at the sideburns. Under his armpits were
large sweat marks. It occurred to Anton as in a fairy tale
that this was the man who had killed Ploeg.

"I was saying something you shouldn't have heard," said

Takes. "But you did hear, and then you said something you didn't mean to say. Those are the facts, and that's why we're sitting here. I knew of your existence. How old were you then?"

"Twelve."

"Did you know him, that pig?"

"Only by sight," said Anton, but the word pig in connection with Ploeg did sound familiar.

"I should think so; he came by your house regularly."

"And I was in the same class as his son." As he said this he didn't remember that boy of long ago, but the big fellow who had thrown a stone into his mirror ten years before.

"Wasn't his name also Fake?"

"Yes."

"There were two other daughters besides. The youngest was four then."

"The same age mine is now."

"So you see, those are not attenuating circumstances." Anton realized he was shivering. He felt in the presence of a nameless violence such as he had never known in anyone, except possibly in that man at the scene of the fire, the Nazi with the scar under his cheekbone. Should he say so? He didn't. He didn't want to give the impression that he was attacking Takes. Besides, it would be nothing new to Takes; clearly he had put such considerations behind him long ago.

"Do you want me to tell you what sort of man this Ploeg was?"

"Not for my sake."

"But for mine. He had a whip with barbed wire braided into it that ripped the skin off your bare ass, which he then shoved against the blazing stove. He put a garden hose up your ass and let it run till you vomited your own shit. He killed God knows how many people, and sent many more to their deaths in Germany and Poland. Very well. So he had to be gotten rid of . . . Do you agree?" And as Anton kept silent, "Yes, or yes?"

"Yes," said Anton.

"Okay. But on the other hand, it was clear to us that there were certain to be reprisals."

"Mr. Takes," Anton interrupted him. "Am I right to assume . . ."

"Call me Gijs."

". . . that you are sitting here justifying yourself for my sake? I'm not criticizing you, after all."

"I'm not justifying myself to you."

"To whom, then?"

"I don't know," he answered impatiently. "Certainly not to myself, or to God, or some such nonsense. God doesn't exist, and perhaps I don't either." With the same index finger that had pulled the trigger, he now flicked away the cigarette butt and looked out over the cemetery. "Do you know who exists? The dead. The friends who have died."

As if to announce that someone was in command after all, a small cloud crept over the sun, making the flowers on the new grave look bleached, as if they were repenting, while the gray of the gravestones became dominant. But the next moment, everything was once more bathed in light. Anton wondered whether the sympathy he felt for the man sitting next to him had an ambiguous source. Through him, Anton was no longer simply a victim; now he was vicariously taking part in the violence of the assault. A victim? Of course he had been a victim, even though he was still alive. Yet at the same time, he felt as if it had all happened to someone else.

Takes had lit another cigarette.

"Good. So we knew there would be reprisals, right? That one of the houses would be set on fire, and that some of the hostages would be shot. Is that a reason for not doing it?"

When he kept silent, Anton looked up.

"Do you expect *me* to give you an answer?"

"Sure."

"I can't do that. I don't know about that."

"Then I'll tell you: the answer is no. If you should tell me that your family would still be alive if we hadn't liquidated Ploeg, you'd be right. That's the truth, but no more. If someone were to say that your family would still be alive if your father had rented another house in another street, that too would be the truth. Then I might be sitting here with someone else . . . although it might have happened in that other street, because maybe Ploeg too might have lived somewhere else. Those are the kinds of truths that don't do us any good. The only truth that's useful is that everyone gets killed by whoever kills them, and by no one else. Ploeg by us, your family by the Germans. If you believe we shouldn't have done it, then you also believe that, in the light of history, the human race shouldn't have existed. Because then all the love and happiness and goodness in this world can't outweigh the life of a single child. Yours, for instance. Is that what you believe?"

Anton, confused, looked at the ground. He didn't quite understand it; he had never really thought about these things. But perhaps Takes never thought about anything else.

"So we did it. We knew . . ."

"You mean that it *does* outweigh it?" Anton asked suddenly.

Takes threw the cigarette at his feet and crushed it with his shoe so thoroughly that only a few shreds remained. These he covered with gravel. He continued without answering the question.

"We knew that probably at least one of those houses would get it. The Fascist gentlemen were rather consistent as far as that goes. But we didn't know which house. We had chosen that spot because it was the most secluded and the easiest to get away from. And we had to get away, for we had a few more scum like that on our list."

Anton said slowly, "If your parents had lived in one of those houses, would you have shot him there?"

Takes stood up, took two steps in his sloppy pants, and turned to him. "No, dammit," he said. "Of course not. What do you mean? Not if it might as well have been done somewhere else. But that same night, you know, my youngest brother happened to be among those hostages. And would you like to know what Mother thought of that? She agreed that I was right to do it. She's still alive; you can ask her. Would you like her address?"

Anton tried to avoid looking at his left eye. "You keep at me as if it were my fault. I was twelve years old and reading a book when it happened, for goodness' sake."

Takes sat down again and lit another cigarette. "It's just a stupid coincidence that it happened in front of your house."

Anton eyed him sideways. "It didn't happen in front of our house," he said.

Slowly Takes turned to face him. "I beg your pardon?"

"It happened in front of a neighbor's house. They put him in front of our house."

Takes stretched his legs, crossed his feet, and put one hand in his pocket. Nodding, he surveyed the cemetery. "Better a good neighbor than a distant friend," he said after a while. He was shaking with something, perhaps laughter. "What kind of people were they?"

"A widower and his daughter. A seaman." Takes once more nodded his head.

"Well, I must say . . . I hadn't thought of that possibility: one can always help fate along a bit."

"And is that morally justifiable?" asked Anton, realizing instantly that it was a childish question.

"Justifiable . . ." repeated Takes. "You'll have to ask the clergyman about that. I believe he's still wandering around here somewhere. Some people simply take justice into their own hands. Go tell them they're wrong to do it. Three seconds later it would have happened in front of your door."

"I'm only asking," said Anton, "because my brother then

tried to move him up one house further, or to put him back where he was . . . I'm not sure, because the police arrived next."

"Jesus, now I'm beginning to understand!" cried Takes. "That's why he was outside. But how did he get hold of that gun?"

Anton looked up at him in surprise. "How do you know about the gun?"

"Because I looked it up after the War, of course."

"It was Ploeg's gun."

"What an instructive afternoon," Takes said slowly. He puffed on his cigarette and blew the smoke out of the corners of his mouth. "Who was living in the next house further down?"

"Two old people." The trembling hand reaching for him. Pickles are just like crocodiles, Mr. Beumer had said. Anton had repeated this once to Sandra, but she didn't laugh; she just agreed.

"Yes," said Takes. "Of course, if he'd put the body back, there would have been a fight." And then right away, "My, my, my, what a clumsy mess. A bunch of fools, all of you, traipsing up and down with that body."

"What else should we have done?"

"Taken it in, of course!" snarled Takes. "You should have dragged him into the house at once."

Anton looked at him, perplexed. Of course! Columbus's egg! Before he had time to say another word, Takes continued, "Just think: they'd heard shots somewhere in the neighborhood. What could they possibly have done about it if they hadn't seen anything on the street? It wouldn't occur to them that a man had been rubbed out, would it? They'd think that one of the militia had taken a shot at someone, maybe. Or were your neighbors collaborators who might have given you away?"

"No. But what would we have done with the body?"

"How should I know? Hidden it. Under the floorboards, or buried in the garden. Or better yet, eaten it up right away—cooked it and shared it with the neighbors. After all, it was the winter of starvation. War criminals don't count, as far as cannibalism is concerned."

Now laughter shook Anton. His father the clerk baking a police inspector and eating him for dinner! *De gustibus non est disputandum.*

"Or were you under the impression that such things never happened? Forget it; everything has happened. The weirdest things you can think of have happened, and weirder yet."

The people strolling back and forth to the grave eyed them in passing, two men on a stone bench under a tree (one younger than the other), still mourning their lost friend while the others were sitting in the bar, exchanging memories: do you remember the time that he . . . As they walked by, they fell thoughtfully silent.

"It's easy for you to say," said Anton. "You thought of nothing else but this sort of thing, whereas we were sitting at home, reading, around the dining-room table, and then suddenly we heard those shots."

"I still would have thought of it at once."

"Maybe, but then you were part of a gang. My father was a clerk who never took action; he just wrote down the actions of others. We wouldn't have had time, anyway. Although . . ." he said, looking up suddenly into the leaves overhead, "we had a kind of quarrel . . ."

In spite of the brilliance of the day, a scene flashed through his mind. Some obscure activity taking place in total darkness, in a hall; an exclamation, as if Peter were stumbling over some branches, something about a key . . . It disappeared like the shred of a dream briefly remembered the next morning.

He was brought back to reality by Takes, who drew four lines in the gravel with his heel, making this design in the bare earth:

"Listen," he said. "There were four houses, weren't there?"

"Yes."

"And you lived in the second house from the left."

"You've got a good memory."

"I go back there now and then. Heroes always return to the scene, it's a well-known fact. Although . . . quite probably I'm the only one, at least as far as that quay of yours is concerned. Now, as far as I knew he was lying here, in front of your house. At which neighbor's was he shot—this one, or this one?"

"This one," said Anton, and pointed with his shoe to the second house from the right.

Takes nodded and looked at the stripes.

"Excuse me, but in that case there's a mystery. Why did the seaman deposit him at your doorstep and not here, at his other neighbor's?"

Anton too looked at the stripes. "No idea. I've never wondered about it."

"There must be a reason. Did he dislike you?"

"Not as far as I know. I used to go there sometimes. I should think they would have been more inclined to dislike the people on the other side, who ignored everybody else on the street."

"And you never tried to find out?" asked Takes, surprised. "Don't you care at all?"

"Care, care . . . I told you, I don't feel any need to go over all that again. What happened happened, and that's all there is to it. It can't be changed now, even if I understood it. It was wartime, one big disaster, my family was murdered, and I've put all that out of my life. I was adopted by an aunt and uncle, and everything turned out all right for me. You were right to kill the bastard, really; I have no complaints about that. You just convince his son! With me that's not necessary, but why in God's name do you want to make it all logical? That's impossible, and who cares? It's history, ancient history. How many times has the same sort of thing happened since? It may be happening right now somewhere, while we're sitting here talking. Could you swear, your hand in the fire, that at this very moment someone's house somewhere isn't being set on fire by a flamethrower? In Vietnam, for instance? What are you talking about? When you took me outside just now, I thought maybe you were concerned about my peace of mind, but that doesn't seem to be the case—at least, not altogether. You're more upset than I am. It seems to me that you can't leave the War alone, but time goes on. Or do you regret what you did?"

He had spoken fast but calmly, yet with the vague feeling that he must be careful, that he must control himself so as not to upset the other.

"I'd do it again tomorrow, if necessary," said Takes without hesitation. "And maybe I will do it again tomorrow. I've rubbed out a whole rat's nest of that scum, and the fact still gives me great satisfaction. But the incident on that quay of yours . . . there was more to it. Something happened there." He clasped the edge of the bench and shifted his position. "Let's just say that I wish we hadn't gone through with it."

"Because my parents were killed as well?"

"No," said Takes roughly. "I'm sorry to say that's not the reason. That couldn't have been foreseen or expected. It probably happened because they caught your brother with a gun, or because of something else, or for no reason; I don't know."

"It probably happened," said Anton without looking up, "because my mother flew at the leader of those Germans."

Takes was silent and stared straight ahead. At last he turned to Anton and said, "I'm really not torturing you just to satisfy my nostalgia for the War, in case you're wondering. I know people like that, but I'm not one of them. Those people spend all their holidays in Berlin and would just love to hang a portrait of Hitler over their beds. No, the problem is that something else happened over there in Haarlem." A light went on in his eyes. Anton saw his Adam's apple bob up and down a couple of times. "Your parents and your brother and those hostages were not the only ones who lost their lives. The fact is that I wasn't alone when I shot Ploeg; there were two of us. Someone was with me—someone who . . . Let's just say she was my girl friend. But never mind, leave it at that."

Anton stared at him, and suddenly all the pent-up emotion washed over him. Putting his face in his hands, he turned away and began to sob. She was dying. For him she died at this very moment, as if twenty-one years were nothing. Yet at the same time she was resurrected together with all she had meant to him, hidden there in the darkness. If he had ever thought about her in these twenty-one years, he would have wondered whether she were still alive. But just now, he realized, he had been looking for her, in the church and later in the café—and in fact it was the reason why he had come to this funeral where he had no need to be.

He felt Takes's hand on his shoulder. "What's this about?" He dropped his hands. His eyes were dry.

"How did she die?"

"They shot her in the dunes, three weeks before Liberation. She's buried there in the memorial cemetery. But why should you care so much?"

"Because I know her," Anton said softly. "Because I talked to her. I spent that night with her in the cell."

Takes looked at him in disbelief. "How do you know it was her? What's her name? Surely she didn't tell you who she was."

"No, but I'm quite sure."

"Did she tell you that she was involved in the assault?"

Anton shook his head. "No, not even that. But I'm quite certain."

"How can you be, for God's sake," Takes said crossly. "What did she look like?"

"I don't know. It was pitch-dark."

Takes thought for a while. "Would you recognize her if you saw a picture?"

"I never really saw her, Takes. But . . . I'd very much like to see her picture."

"But what did she say? You must know *something*!"

Anton shrugged. "I wish I did. It was so long ago . . . She had been wounded."

"Where?"

"I don't know."

Tears came to Takes's eyes. "It must have been her," he said. "If she didn't even mention her name . . . Ploeg took a final shot at her, just as we were about to turn the corner."

When Anton saw Takes's tears he began to weep himself.

"What was her name?" he asked.

"Truus. Truus Coster." Now the people around the grave were watching them, discreetly but steadily. They must have been surprised to see two grown men so much affected by the death of a friend. Some may have wondered if they were showing off.

"There they are, the silly fools." His mother-in-law's voice. She entered the gate—two figures in black and a child in white against the blinding gravel. Sandra called "Papa!" dropped her doll, and ran toward Anton. He picked her up and held her in his arms. From Saskia's wide-eyed look he could tell that she was worried about him, and he nodded to her reassuringly. But her mother, leaning on her shiny black cane with the silver handle, would not be fobbed off that easily.

"Good Lord, are they actually crying?" she asked angrily,

at which Sandra looked up at Anton. Mrs. De Graaff pretended to gag. "You two make me positively ill. Can't you stop carrying on about that rotten War? Tell me, Gijs, do you enjoy torturing my son-in-law? Yes, of course, you would." She gave a strange, mocking laugh and her wobbly cheeks shook. "This is impossible, the way you two stand there like two exposed necrophiliacs, and in the cemetery, of all places. Stop it at once. Come along, all of you."

She turned about and walked away, pointing at the doll that lay on the gravel, not doubting for a minute that she would be obeyed. And so she was.

"Isn't she amazing?" said Takes, also with a peculiar laugh. It was evident that he'd dealt with her before, and at Anton's puzzled look he said, "Queen Wilhelmina."

As they walked back to the square, the child told them that she had gone with her mother to the house of that dead man and had been given two glasses of orangeade. The café was emptying. At the entrance stood the car with the official insignia, its driver stationed by the back door. Anton was being closely observed, but no one bothered him. Sandra and her mother went into the café to fetch De Graaff. Saskia, the doll in her hands, said that Sandra absolutely must have something to eat. She had already suggested to Mrs. De Graaff that they have lunch together somewhere in the country.

"Just stand still a minute," said Takes.

Anton felt Takes scribbling something on his back. Saskia was once more observing him with a worried look, and he closed his eyes for an instant to signal her that he was all right. Takes tore a sheet out of his diary, folded it, and put it in Anton's breast pocket. In silence they shook hands. He nodded to Saskia and went into the café.

By the sidewalk Jaap was starting up his scooter. Just as he managed it, the minister and De Graaff came out. The driver took off his cap and opened the door. But first the minister went to Jaap and shook his hand.

"See you soon, Jaap."

"Yes," said Jaap. "Until next time, I guess."

Sandra, of course, wanted to ride in the car with Grandma and Grandpa, so as their car followed Anton's along small country roads to a restaurant he had heard of, he could have talked undisturbed with Saskia about what had happened. Yet he sat behind the wheel in silence. Saskia, who had been brought up not to ask questions when people who had been through the War turned up, inquired only whether it had been some sort of reconciliation scene. "Something like that," he answered, even though it wasn't really true. He kept his eyes on the road. Feeling as if he had soaked too long in a hot bath, he tried to go over his conversation with Takes. But he was not quite ready for it yet, as if so far there were nothing to think about. He remembered the piece of paper that Takes had slipped into his pocket. Pulling it out, he unfolded it with the fingers of one hand and saw a scribbled address and telephone number.

"Are you going to look him up?" asked Saskia.

He put it back in his pocket and smoothed his hair to the side.

"I don't think so," he said.

"But you're not throwing it away."

He smiled at her. "True, I'm not."

About ten minutes later they reached the restaurant, a converted, steep-roofed farmhouse of a solidly provincial pretentiousness. Inside it was dark and empty. Meals were being served in the shaded orchard by waiters in tailcoats.

"I want french fries," Sandra cried as she came running from the other car.

"French fries!" repeated Mrs. De Graaff and once more she pretended to gag. "I find that vulgar." And to Saskia, "Can't you teach the child to call them *pommes frites*?"

"Let the poor kid eat french fries," said De Graaff, "if she doesn't like *pommes frites*."

"I want french fries."

"You'll get your french fries," De Graaff said, covering her head with his hand as if it were a helmet. "With scrambled eggs. Or do you prefer *oeufs brouillés*?"

"No, scrambled eggs."

"Come on, Dad," said Saskia. "That'll do."

De Graaff seated himself at the head of the table and again clasped its edge with outstretched arms. When the waiter handed him the menu, he pushed it aside with the back of his hand.

"Fish for the man. French fries and scrambled eggs for the young lady, and some Chablis in an ice cooler frosted on the outside. When I look at you in your hot uniform, I'll enjoy my wine all the more." Waiting till his wife suppressed a giggle, he draped the napkin over his lap. "You know the anecdote about Dickens, don't you? Every Christmas Eve he gave a party for his friends. The fire was lit, the candles burning, and as they sat around their roast goose, they would hear outside the window, in the snow, a lonely wanderer stamping his feet and waving his arms to keep warm. Every now and then the poor man would exclaim, 'Ho hum hum, what bitter cold!' He was of course hired for the purpose, to emphasize the contrast."

He laughed at Anton, who sat across from him. His cheerfulness was evidently meant to be of help, but his laughter faded when he saw the look in Anton's eyes. He put the napkin down next to his plate, beckoned with his head, and stood up. Anton followed him. Sandra also rose, but Mrs. De Graaff said, "Stay here."

The two men came to a stop by the side of a ditch full of duckweed that separated the yard from the meadow.

"How are things, Anton?"

"I'll be all right, Father."

"That damned fool Gijs. What a first-class blunderer! During the War he was tortured and never said a word, and now he's shooting his mouth off all over the place. How in heaven's name did you end up next to him at the table?"

"In a way, it was the second time our paths crossed," said Anton.

De Graaff looked puzzled. "Yes, I suppose so," he said when he understood.

"But that's why it fits. I mean . . . It completes the picture."

"It completes the picture," De Graaff repeated, nodding. "Well, well, you speak in riddles, but I suppose that's your way of getting it off your chest."

Anton laughed. "I don't quite know myself what I mean."

"Yes, but then who's supposed to understand? Never mind; the important thing is to keep it under control. Perhaps it was a lucky thing for you that it happened this afternoon. We've been suppressing it all these years—and now come the problems. I hear it from all sides. Twenty years seems to be a kind of incubation period for our disease; all that unrest in Amsterdam must have something to do with it."

"I can't say you give the impression of having any problems."

"Yes . . ." said De Graaff, digging with the tip of his shoe at a pebble stuck between the weeds. "Yes . . ." Unable to loosen the stone, he looked up at Anton and nodded. "Let's go back to the table. Don't you think that's best?"

After the De Graaffs had driven off to Gelderland, Saskia and Anton took turns going to the bathroom and returned in beach clothes. Having completed this metamorphosis, they drove to Wijk-aan-Zee.

At the end of the narrow road through the dunes, where old bunkers, the former Atlantic fortifications, were still scattered here and there, the sea stretched out smooth and tamèd as far as the horizon. Since it was an ordinary school day, the beach was occupied mostly by mothers with small children. They walked on bare feet through the hot sand and the brittle, sharp row of shells between the tidemark and the first line of waves. Not till there did it finally cool down.

Saskia and Sandra immediately stripped to their bathing suits and ran to the lukewarm tidal pool in front of the first sandbank. Anton tidied their belongings: spread out the towels, tucking a detective story beneath them, folded the clothes, set out a pail and shovel, and put his watch in Saskia's pocketbook. Then he entered the water slowly, walking toward the deep.

Beyond the second sandbar, where he no longer touched bottom, the water became really cold. Yet it was a strange, unpleasant cold that seemed to rise out of the still, dead deep, penetrating his body without refreshing it. He swam about for a while. Though less than two hundred meters offshore, he no longer felt as if he belonged to the land. The coast—dunes, a lighthouse, low buildings with high antennas—stretched out in silence to the right and left, a world fundamentally different from the one he was in now. Suddenly he felt tired and alone, and his teeth began to chatter. He swam back as fast as he could, as if to escape a terrible danger that lay beyond the horizon. Gradually the sea grew warmer, and as soon as he touched ground he waded to the shore. Near Saskia and Sandra it was as warm as bath water. Here he stretched out on his back on the hard ridges of sand, spread his arms, and gave a deep sigh.

"It's cold farther out," he said.

Back on the beach he pulled his towel a few meters higher up where the white sand was hot. Saskia sat down next to him and together they watched Sandra, who herself was eyeing a little girl her own age building a sand castle. After a while Sandra too began to dig. The other girl pretended not to notice.

"How do you feel?" asked Saskia. He put his arm around her shoulders.

"Fine."

"Can't you forget it?"

"I have forgotten." He turned over on his stomach. "The sun feels good." He hid his face in the hollow of his arm and closed his eyes. With a chill he felt a trickle running onto his back and side, and then Saskia's hands oiling him . . .

A little later, lifting his head with a start, he knew that he must have dozed off. He sat up again and watched Saskia on her knees rubbing oil into Sandra, who paid no attention. The sun was at its hottest. A ball was being tossed back and forth in the water, and two boys were playing the guitar under a canvas awning. Tiny children ran in and out of the sea and poured their pails of water into holes in the sand, with the unshakable conviction that the water would eventually stay. Anton picked up his book and tried to read, but without sunglasses, he was blinded by the glare of the paper, even when it was shaded by his head.

Sandra began to whine, and Saskia took her back into the water. When they emerged they walked, dripping, to a crowd that had gathered farther down, but a minute later Sandra came running in tears to Anton. Boys over there, she told him, were hacking with shovels at a purple jellyfish as big as a pancake, and the jellyfish was unable to fight back.

With a determination like her mother's, Saskia began to gather her possessions. "I'm going shopping with Sandra in the village, and after that we'll go home. She's dead-tired. First the church, then the burial, and then the visit to the widow's house . . ." Crouching, she rubbed Sandra dry till the child stood shaking on her little legs.

"Let me come along, then."

"No, please. Stay here; otherwise, it'll just take longer. We'll drink something and then come back to fetch you."

He followed them with his eyes in order to wave at them once more, but they trudged up the beach without turning back. When they had disappeared he lay down on his back, glistening with sweat.

Gradually the sounds of the beach withdrew to the outer rim of a bowl as wide as heaven. He himself was floating like a dot at its center, in an empty, rose-colored space that was rapidly receding from the world. Something was beginning to pulse underground somewhere, and yet there was no ground. Space itself was pulsing, thumping. It grew darker and cloudy, as when a drop of ink falls into a glass of water: a gradual mingling which will not blend, a spreading like plasma, a transformation, so that a vague hand turns into an old-fashioned professor's face with a goatee and a monocle, and then into a harnessed circus elephant riding a flatbed. The thumping becomes that of a train in a railroad station full of switches; the train vanishes in waves of music, rippling the wheat. All grows darker as night dribbles down. Above the feathered helmet of a suit of armor, a flame still flickers. Then everything grows hard, indestructible, and the light returns, a giant, rose-colored crystal door, not lit up by the light, but the source of it. Above it, two angels with garlands of lobed leaves, also made of crystal. The door has been locked with built-in or melted-in iron bars, painted pink. Nothing has changed in all these years, he notices. He is home again in Carefree. Though the doors are barred, he enters, but the rooms are empty. Everything has been transformed; there are multitudes of statues, sculptures, ornaments. It is silent, as in the depths of the sea. He wades through the rooms (which have grown into vast halls) with difficulty, as if he is being held back by something. With a flash of recognition he comes upon his father's small study at the back of the house. But where the slanting wall used to be, there is now a glass addition like a large hothouse or winter garden, and inside it is a little fountain and the elegant, chalk-white facade of a Greek temple . . .

Alone, he lay on the sofa in his underwear, the doors of the balcony wide open to the summer evening. The room was lit only by the late twilight and the street lamps. Only now did the deep sunburn on his face and the front of his legs begin to show. It was unusual for his slightly olive complexion to burn at all, but he was as red as if he'd had a terrible beating. When Sandra had shaken him awake at the beach, he'd been asleep for more than an hour. In sleep the blood circulates more slowly, whereas in the sun it is supposed to move faster to counteract the heat—and so sleepers get sunburned. He had awakened with a splitting headache, but in the back of the car, in the soothing shade, it had almost disappeared. No doubt the wine at lunch had something to do with it.

The continuous murmur of traffic sounded in the distance, but from the street itself came only the voices of some people sitting on a balcony or downstairs on the stoop. A child was playing the recorder a few houses away. Because Sandra couldn't get to sleep, Saskia put her down on their double bed after dinner and lay down next to her. Then Saskia too immediately fell asleep.

Stretched on the sofa, Anton stared straight ahead. He was thinking of Takes, of how everything comes to light sooner or later, and is dealt with and then laid aside. How long ago was it that he visited the Beumers? Some fifteen years, more than the age he had been in 1945. No doubt Mr. Beumer now lay in his coffin, and Mrs. Beumer as well. He hadn't been to Haarlem since. And Fake, God knows where he was; it didn't matter. Perhaps he was running the business in Den Helder by now. But with Takes it was different: they had wept together. It was the first time that he had cried over what had happened, yet it wasn't because of his parents, or Peter, but because a girl had died. He had never seen Truus . . . Truus what? He raised himself and tried to think of her last name, but couldn't. Shot in the dunes; blood on the sand.

He closed his eyes to recall the darkness of the cell, her fingers softly caressing his face. He covered his face with his hands and peered wide-eyed through the bars of his fingers. He breathed deeply and brushed his hair back with both hands. He shouldn't be doing this, it was dangerous. There was something wrong with him. He should go to bed. But he crossed his arms and went on staring straight ahead.

Takes had a picture of her. Should Anton go to him and identify her? She had been Takes's girl friend, his great love, apparently, and obviously he had the right to a last message from her. Anton couldn't remember anything she had said, only that she had talked a lot and touched his face. All he would accomplish by going would be to eradicate that great anonymous presence and restore her to a particular face. Was that what he wanted? Wouldn't it diminish what she still meant to him? It didn't matter whether her face had been beautiful or ugly, attractive or unattractive or whatever, but if he saw her picture it would acquire one definite aspect and no other. Now he had no image of her at all, only an abstract awareness, such as Catholic children have of their guardian angel.

And then what happened was this: Moving the way a weightless trapeze artist rises from the safety net into which he has fallen, he rose from his prone position onto his knees. There he confronted the photograph he had been staring at all this time without realizing it. It stood, framed, together with his collection of sextants on the mahogany cabinet decorated with brass. In the deep twilight it was difficult to make the picture out, but he knew it well: Saskia in a black dress down to her ankles, her belly big with Sandra, who would be born a few days later. It was not true that he had never imagined what the woman whose name seemed to be

Truus looked like. From the very beginning he had imagined her looking like this and not otherwise—like Saskia. This was what he had recognized in Saskia at first sight that afternoon at the Stone of Scone. She was the embodiment of an image he must have been carrying about in his head, without knowing it, since he was twelve. Her appearance revealed it to him—not as something remembered, but as immediate love, immediate certainty that she must remain with him and carry his child.

Worried, he began to pace the room. What kind of thoughts were these? Perhaps it was true, perhaps not, but if it should be true, wasn't he doing something peculiar to Saskia? She was, after all, someone in her own right. What was her connection with a girl from the Resistance who had been shot long ago? If she was not allowed to be herself but represented someone else, then wasn't he in the process of breaking up his marriage? She would never have a chance, for she couldn't be someone else. In a sense, he was involved in murdering her.

On the other hand, he wouldn't be married to Saskia now if he hadn't met that girl under the police headquarters. Then the two women had become indistinguishable, that is to say, his imagination was still busy combining them. For probably Saskia didn't look like Truus, since he had no idea what Truus looked like. Besides, Takes would have reacted differently to Saskia, and he had paid hardly any attention to her. Saskia only looked like the image which Truus had aroused in his, Anton's, imagination. But where did this image come from? Perhaps it originated with a much more ancient source; perhaps it came—in the manner of Freud—from the image he had of his mother while he was still in the cradle.

He stood on the balcony and looked out unseeing. Whenever he was told in the hospital that a new colleague with such-and-such a name would be arriving the following day, he would begin immediately to visualize that person. The imagined image never agreed with the person's actual appearance, but where did these notions come from? The same was true with famous authors and artists: when he saw their photographs for the first time, he was often terribly surprised. Without being aware of it, he'd had a preconceived notion of their appearance. Sometimes he lost all interest in the person's work after seeing the photograph. This was the case with Joyce, for instance, and not because he was ugly. Sartre was much uglier, but his portrait had increased Anton's interest. Apparently the preconceived notion was sometimes more accurate than the reality.

In other words, there was nothing wrong with Saskia's looking like his idea of Truus. Truus had, under those circumstances, aroused an image in his mind to which Saskia seemed to respond, and that was fine, for it was not Truus's image, but his own, and where it came from was unimportant. Besides, maybe the whole thing really worked in reverse. Saskia had touched his heart at first glance, and perhaps this was why, in retrospect, he decided that Truus must have looked the same way. But in that case he was being unfair to Truus, and therefore it was his duty to know not only her name, but also what she actually looked like: she, Truus Coster.

It was cooling off. Police sirens sounded in the distance. Something was happening again in the city, as things had been happening for almost a year now. It was ten-thirty, and he decided to call Takes at once. He went upstairs to the bedroom. Here too the curtain was still open. The blankets were thrown back, and Sandra lay sleeping under the sheet with her mouth wide open. Saskia, half undressed, lay on her stomach, one arm around the child. He stood watching them for a moment in the warm silence filled with sleep. He had the feeling of having just skirted something fatal, something that now seemed to him a dangerous confusion, dizzying cerebral cobwebs caused by sunstroke. He must forget them and go to sleep.

Instead, he went to look for his jacket, which Saskia had thrown over a chair. With the vague sense that he was still courting danger, he used two fingers to fish the slip of paper out of his breast pocket.

5

"Anytime," Takes said. "Why not come right now?" When Anton excused himself because he had a slight headache, Takes answered, "Who doesn't?" The next day Anton would be on duty till four, so they made a date for four-thirty.

The heat continued. He had trouble concentrating on his work. When it was over he was glad to get outside and walk to the Nieuwe Zijds Voorburgwal. The sunburn on his face and chest was still painful. While Saskia had been thoroughly oiling him once more that morning, he had wondered whether to tell her about his appointment, but decided against it. On the Spui stood a detachment of blue police squad cars. Tension hung about the city, but it had become routine. The mayor and the minister would take care of it.

Takes lived in a shabby, narrow house behind the Royal Palace on the Dam, in a side street that only delivery trucks were allowed to enter. The house dated from more prosperous times, and on its gable was a stone relief representing a kind of mythical beast with a fish in its mouth. The inscription underneath said THE OTTER. On the front stoop it took a while before Anton found the right name among all the different offices and private apartments. Takes's was penciled on a scrap of paper thumbtacked under a bell, along with instructions to ring three times.

When Takes opened the door, Anton saw at once that he'd been drinking. His eyes were watery and his face blotchier than the day before. He was unshaven: a grayish film covered his jaws and neck down to his open shirt. Anton followed him through a narrow hall with peeling plaster, parked bicycles, boxes, pails, and a half-deflated rubber boat. Behind closed doors, the clatter of typewriters and a radio. An ancient, winding oak staircase came down at an angle into the hall. Sitting on one of the steps an old man wearing a pajama top over his pants was dismantling a bike pedal.

"Did you read the papers?" asked Takes without looking back.

"Not yet."

In the back of the house through a door at the end of the hall, Takes entered a small room that served as bedroom, study, and kitchen. It contained an unmade bed, as well as something like a desk covered with letters, bank statements, newspapers, and magazines. Jumbled among the papers were a coffee cup, an overflowing ashtray, an open jam pot, and even a shoe. Anton could not bear this confusion of unassorted objects; at home he was unhappy if Saskia left a comb or glove lying on his desk for a minute. The room was littered with pots, pans, unwashed dishes, even suitcases, as if Takes were on the verge of leaving. Above the sink an open window overlooked an untidy yard, where more music was playing. Takes took up a newspaper that was spread out on the bed and folded it over and over until nothing was visible except one front-page article.

"This will interest you too," he said, and Anton saw a headline:

WILLY LAGES
—seriously ill—
RELEASED!

He knew this much, that Lages had been the head of the Gestapo in the Netherlands, and as such was responsible for thousands of executions and the deportation of hundreds of thousands of Jews. After the War he was condemned to death, but the sentence had been commuted to imprisonment a few years later. There had been mass demonstrations, in which Anton had not taken part.

"What do you think of that?" asked Takes. "Because he's *sick*, our dear little Willy. You'll see how soon he recovers back in Germany. And yet he made a lot of other people *really* sick—but that's not so important. All those humane do-gooders with their respect for human life at our expense. The war criminal is sick, oh dear, the poor lamb. Free the Fascist quickly, for we're no Fascists, our hands are clean. Does this make his victims ill? What a hateful lot, those anti-Fascists—they're no better themselves! That's what they'll say next, you'll see. And who'll be the first to approve of this release? All those who kept their hands clean during the War—Catholics in the lead, of course. It's not for nothing that he converted to Catholicism the minute he went to prison. But if he gets to heaven, then I prefer hell . . ." Takes looked at Anton and took the paper out of his hands. "You're just resigned to it, aren't you? I'll assume that you're blushing with shame. Your parents and your brother also came under the jurisdiction of that gentleman."

"Not the wreck he is now."

"The wreck!" Takes took his cigarette out of his mouth, and leaving it open, slowly exhaled the smoke. "Just hand him to me and I'll slit his throat. With a pocketknife, if necessary. The wreck . . . As if it were a question of his physique!" He threw the newspaper on the desk, kicked an empty bottle under the bed, and looked up with a forced laugh. "But you, your profession is to rescue ailing mankind, right?"

"How did you know?" Anton asked, surprised.

"Because I called up your scoundrel of a father-in-law. A man should know who he's dealing with, don't you agree?"

Anton nodded, keeping an eye on him, and a smile crept over his face. "The War is still on; right, Takes?"

"Sure," said Takes and did not evade his eyes. "Sure."

Anton felt ill at ease under the scrutiny of that left eye.

Were they playing a game, waiting to see who would be the first to blink? He lowered his eyes. "And you?" he asked, looking about. "I've been foolish enough not to call anyone. How do you earn a living?"

"In me you see a distinguished mathematician."

Anton burst out laughing. "You've got a pretty messy office for a mathematician."

"That mess came with the War. Since then I survive thanks to a pension from the Foundation Nineteen Forty–Forty-five. It was founded by Mr. A. Hitler, who rescued me from mathematics. Without him I'd still be facing the classroom every day." He took a bottle of whisky from the windowsill and poured some for Anton. "Let's drink to compassion for the pitiless," he said and raised his glass. "Cheers."

Anton knew the lukewarm whisky would not agree with him, but refusing it was out of the question. Takes was more cynical than yesterday, perhaps because of the newspaper article or the drinking, or maybe he had simply decided to get into this mood. He didn't offer a seat, and for some reason this pleased Anton. Why should people always have to sit? After all, Clemenceau had even had himself buried on his feet. They stood facing each other in the small room, glasses in hand, as at a cocktail party.

"As a matter of fact, I too worked in the medical line," said Takes.

"Really? So we're colleagues?"

"You might call it that."

"Tell me," said Anton, apprehensive.

"Let's just say it was sort of an anatomical institute, somewhere in Holland. The director had put it at our disposal to further the good cause. People were tried there, death penalties were pronounced, and so on. They were executed, too."

"That's little known."

"Shouldn't be. You never know when you'll need it again.

It was mostly for people within the Resistance—traitors in our ranks, infiltrators, that sort. Downstairs in the cellar they were given a phenol injection straight into the heart, with a long needle. Afterwards they were cut into slices on a granite counter by other white-clad heroes. Ears, hands, noses, penises, and intestines floated in a large basin filled with formaldehyde. It would be very hard to piece them together again. All for the benefit of science, you understand!" He faced Anton defiantly. "You see, I'm a worthless son of a bitch."

"So long as it's for a good cause . . ." said Anton.

"The Krauts were scared of that institute, they did their best to avoid it . . . They thought it was pretty spooky."

"But not you."

"Downstairs there were rows of steel cabinets with drawers, about five drawers each, and in every one a corpse. I spent a night in there once, when I had to disappear for a while."

"And? Did you sleep well?"

"Like a log."

"May I ask you something, Takes?"

"Go ahead, laddie," said Takes, smiling sweetly.

"What exactly are you doing this for? Do you think I have to be initiated, or something? That's not really necessary. I've had my share, and no one knows it better than you."

Takes kept his eyes on him as he took another sip.

"I want you to be aware of the man you're dealing with, too." His eyes still on Anton, he took the bottle. "Come, leave the door open for the telephone." Anton followed him to the basement, where there was another hall. With a key Takes unlocked a door that opened into a low room whose function was unclear. It was stuffy. The dim light entering through the basement windows was supplemented by the cold glare of fluorescent tubes that flickered feebly with purplish flashes. The chipped white tiles against the wall suggested that this used to be the kitchen of a private home.

Along the low ceiling ran all kinds of pipes and heating ducts. A low table with another well-filled ashtray stood in the middle of the room, and against the long wall, a worn-out red velvet sofa. There was also an old-fashioned linen closet with a mirror on its door, and a wreck of a bicycle.

The whole had the air of a bunker, an underground headquarters, especially with the torn, yellowed map taped to the wall across from the sofa. Glass in hand, Anton went toward it. "Topography of Germany" was written on the lower right-hand corner. The map was covered with red and blue lines like tidal waves, showing offensives advancing from Russia and France toward Berlin, where they met. The only uncolored areas were north and central Germany and the western part of the Netherlands. His attention was caught by something floating over the faded blue of the sea: a faint, pale-pink outline of a mouth, a kiss printed on the paper with lipstick. He turned around. Takes, sitting cross-legged on the sofa, was watching him.

"So that's how it is," Takes said.

Was this the reason why the map was hanging here? Not because of an insidious nostalgia for the War, but because her mouth was imprinted on it? Was the basement a memorial? But perhaps she and the War had become one for Takes. Perhaps the War had become his beloved, and for that reason he could not be unfaithful to her. Perhaps even as he was talking about its atrocities, he was really trying to remember Truus Coster and those days when he had been happy.

Involuntarily, though there was room enough to stand upright, Anton lowered his head. He sat down next to Takes and looked again at the mouth rising from the North Sea. It was as if the rest of her face were under water. (As a boy he used to imagine that if he looked at the map of Holland under a microscope, he would be able to see the people of Haarlem walking around in the street, and even to see himself leaning over the microscope, if he were doing it outside in the garden.) The fair Ophelia . . . Her lips had touched that spot on the map, perhaps while she and Takes were filling in the lines showing the fronts with the help of news from Radio London, and while they were making plans about what they would do after the Liberation . . . He heard Takes clearing his throat. But Takes poured himself another drink, a cigarette hanging from his lips, and remained silent. Anton had never felt so involved with another man, and maybe the same was true of Takes. From outside came the gentle tune of a carillon. Anton looked at the bicycle, a man's model with a crossbar and the kind of seat you don't see nowadays. It used to be called a Terrysaddle.

Then he saw the photograph.

It was shaped like a postcard and stuck behind an electric cable not far from the map. His heart began to pound. Motionless he stared at the face looking at him across a span of twenty years. After a while he glanced at Takes, who was watching the smoke rising from his mouth. Then he stood up and walked toward it.

Saskia. It was Saskia looking at him. Of course, it wasn't Saskia, it didn't even look like her, but the expression in the eyes was Saskia's, just as it had struck him that first time in Westminster Abbey. A not unusual, friendly girl of twenty-three. The smile drew her mouth a bit to the right side of her face, giving it a certain sophistication. It contrasted with her prim, high-collared dress that had a little embroidered detail in front and the hint of a puffed sleeve. She had thick, wavy hair down to her shoulders; probably light-brown hair, but one couldn't tell from the black-and-white print. The edges were overexposed, so that rebellious streaks of light curled and flashed around her head against the dark background.

Now Takes was standing next to him.

"Is it her?"

"It must be, it must be . . ." said Anton without taking his eyes off it.

Finally she had risen out of the darkness—with Saskia's eyes. He remembered his worries of the night before, but was too excited to realize what this likeness meant. Besides, Takes didn't let him. As if he had controlled himself desperately till now, he seized Anton by the shoulders and shook him the way a teacher might do to the child who has fallen asleep.

"Tell me, what else did she say?"

"I can't remember."

"Did she mention me?"

"I don't remember, Takes."

"Well, try to, for Chrissake!"

Shouting gave Takes a coughing fit that sent him to the corner of the room. Bent over, almost throwing up, he stood supporting himself with his hands on his knees. When he straightened up breathless, Anton said, "It's all gone, Takes. I wish I could tell you, but the only thing I remember is that she touched my face. Later there was blood on it, and that's how I knew that she'd been wounded. Don't forget that I was only twelve. I can't even remember my own father's voice. Our house had just been set on fire; my parents, my brother had disappeared. I was in shock. I was hungry, sitting in a dark cell under a police station."

"A police station?" Takes stared at him open-mouthed. "Which police station?"

"In Heemstede."

Takes made a desperate move with his arm. "So that's where she was. Jesus, we could have gotten her out of there. I thought it was in Haarlem."

At that very moment, Anton could tell, a plan was forming in Takes's head to infiltrate police headquarters in Heemstede. He turned away and paced angrily up and down. The memory of the conversation had disappeared, permanently vanished from the world. He knew that experiments with LSD were going on at the University. It was stored somewhere in his brain, of course. Serious candi-

139

dates for the experiment were welcome, and the drug might make it come back. If Takes knew, he might be crazy enough to insist that Anton go through with the experiment. But Anton had no desire to; he did not want his past chemically resurrected. Besides, there was the risk that none of these memories would be revealed—that totally different, unexpected ones would emerge instead, and that he would not be able to control them.

"All I remember," he said, "is that she told a long story about something."

"About what?"

"I can't remember."

"Jesus Christ!" Takes emptied his glass and slid it across the table like a bartender in a Western movie. "I can't remember, I can't remember!"

Anton remained standing. "What you'd like best," he said, "would be to tie me to a chair, aim a lamp at my face, and then try to pull it out of me, right?"

Takes looked down at his feet. "Okay," he said.

There was no need for Anton to gaze at the photograph any longer to know what Truus Coster had looked like. Her face was indelibly printed in his memory.

"Were you married?" he asked.

Takes poured himself another and handed the bottle to Anton.

"I was married, all right, but not to her. I had a wife and two children, about the same age you were, a bit younger, maybe. But she was the one I loved, though she didn't love me. I would have left my family just like that for her, but she only laughed when I suggested it. Whenever I said I loved her, she thought I was just being silly, that it was only because we'd gone through so much together. Anyway, I'm divorced now."

He began to pace the floor. The seat of his pants hung way below his crotch; the backs of the legs were frayed. Anton thought, here's all that's left of the Resistance, a sloppy, unhappy drunk in a basement that he probably never leaves except to bury his friends, while war criminals are being freed and history ignores him.

"A long story," said Takes. "She was good at that, long stories. All the talk . . . We'd sit chewing the fat for hours, always about morality. Also, sometimes about what it would be like after the War, but then she wouldn't say much. Once she told me that when she thought about after the War, it seemed as if she were looking into a deep hole. But whenever we discussed morality, she was in her element. Once I asked her, 'If a Nazi says that he'll shoot either your mother or your father, that you have to choose which one, or else he'll shoot both, what do you do?'

"I had heard of such a case," Takes said, and threw his butt in the ashtray. "She asked me what *I* would do. I said I'd count the buttons on his uniform: father, mother, father, mother . . . The only way to counter inhumanity is with idiocy. But she said she wouldn't tell him anything. Anyone suggesting such a compromise wouldn't keep his word anyway, she thought. Then possibly he might *not* shoot them. But if you said, 'My father,' maybe he *would* shoot your father and then tell you that it had been your choice. And according to her, that would be true, in a way. It was clever of her. It was first-rate, first-rate. Nights on end, we'd sit and talk about our work. Just imagine us sitting there, both of us condemned to death . . ."

"Had you been condemned to death?" asked Anton.

Takes laughed. "Of course; aren't you? Once," he continued, "she had to go home in the middle of the night, long after curfew. She got lost in the dark and sat down on the street somewhere till dawn."

Anton leaned his head back as if he could hear a sound remembered from somewhere, a faint signal that instantly died.

"Till dawn? Somewhere on the street? It's as if I dreamed something like that once."

"She was completely disoriented. Even you must remember how dark it got in those days."

"Yes," said Anton. "It made me want to become an astronomer."

Takes nodded but hardly seemed to hear.

"She thought about things. She was ten years younger than me, but she thought much more than I did. Compared to her I was just a peasant, a kind of mathematical idiot. One day I suggested that we kidnap the children of our dear Reichskommissar Seyss-Inquart, so we could exchange them for several hundred of our own people. But she asked what on earth made me think such a thing? Was I crazy? What did those children have to do with it? True, what did they have to do with it? Nothing at all, of course, not a thing. Just about as much as the Jewish kids that were being mass-murdered. Which means, nothing at all. But that's just the point: you had to attack your enemy where he was most vulnerable, and if that meant his children—and naturally that's what it meant—then you had to get him through his children. And what if the deal didn't go through? Then, of course, the children would have to be sacrificed. Painlessly, in the anatomical institute." He threw a glance at Anton out of the corners of his eyes. "Yes, I'm sorry. I'm a worthless son of a bitch."

"That's the second time you've said so."

"Ach, is that right?" Takes said, acting surprised. "Did I really? Well then, let's say I'm not even worthy of a bitch, shall we? So we didn't go through with it. Fight Fascists with Fascism is my idea, because they don't understand any other language. I'd like to use that as my motto, but in Latin. I'm sure you could translate it perfectly, you intellectual!"

"Fascists with Fascism," Anton said. "You can't put it into Latin. Fasces means a bundle of arrows. 'Bundles of arrows against a bundle of arrows'—it doesn't work."

"There you have it," said Takes. "Truus didn't think it did either. According to her, I had to watch out not to become like them, because that would be their way to get the better of me. Yes, she was a philosopher, Steenwijk; but still, a philosopher with a gun."

He walked past the linen closet, leaned over, opened a drawer, put a big revolver on the table, and walked on as if nothing had happened.

Frightened, Anton gazed at the grayish object that had suddenly appeared. It was so menacing that it seemed likely to singe the table. He looked up.

"Is that her gun?"

"That's her gun."

Motionless, the thing lay there like a relic from a different civilization unearthed by archeologists.

"Did she shoot Ploeg with it?"

"And hit her target," Takes said, pointing his finger at Anton. Takes stared at the gun for a while; clearly it brought something else to his mind. "I was stupidly preoccupied that night," he said, half to himself. "We were riding next to each other on that quay of yours, hand in hand, very slowly, looking as best we could like a pair of lovers. That is . . . as far as I was concerned, we really were. We let him overtake us, and he looked at us for a minute. 'Good morning to you,' Truus called out cheerfully, and he smiled back at us. Then I rode ahead. I had decided to do him in at once, but it was slippery. I had to let go of the handlebar with one hand to pull the gun out of my pocket, and then I skidded. I shot him in the back, and a bit later in the stomach, but I saw right away that it was no good. As he fell to the ground I wanted to try once more, but I misfired. I went on fast, to make way for Truus. When I looked back, I saw her carefully steadying herself with the tip of her shoe on the sidewalk and aiming precisely between his shoulder blades. He lay completely rolled into a ball, his head hidden between his arms. She shot twice, stuck the gun back in her pocket, and quickly rode on. Apparently she was sure that he was dead, but I saw him raise himself up. I screamed at her to watch out, she accelerated, and then he took a shot at her—and by some idiotic accident hit her, somewhere low in her back."

It was as if the gun on the table were a weight that dragged Anton along with it into the depths of the past. Just as he had completely forgotten what happened later in the cell, so he clearly remembered that last evening at home: the shots, and then the empty quay with Ploeg's body. He had known all along, of course, that someone must have been on the quay minutes before the shots sounded, but only in an abstract way, whereas now it became a reality. The scream he heard hadn't been Ploeg's, then, but Takes's. He could have sworn it had been the scream of a dying man.

In the ashtray next to the gun something began to smoulder.

"And then?" he asked.

"And then—and then—and then . . ." said Takes, taking some odd dance steps. "'Once upon a time, they lived happily ever after.' You're just like a child . . . And then she was unable to go on. I tried to hoist her onto my baggage rack, and after that to hide the two of us in the bushes. But when the Germans appeared, a woman called from a window and told them where we were. Truus gave me her gun and a kiss, and that was that. A bit more shooting, and I was off. I tried to find that bitch again before the end of the War, to deal with her on my own terms. She's still around somewhere, pretending to be a dear little old grandmother." He took the gun from the table and weighed it in his hand, the way an antique dealer would handle a precious jewel. "I would have loved to confront her with this. 'Good evening, madam, how are things? All well with the children?'"

He surrounded the trigger with his finger and examined the weapon from all sides. "It can still be used for shooting, you know that? After the War, your father-in-law and his buddies would have liked me to hand it in. I'm under surveillance these days. You're only allowed to keep it as a souvenir, but then you have to have it spiked, so it can't be used. I decided not to. You can never tell when you're going to need it one last time." He put it down and lifted a finger. "Do you hear? It's crying a little. No mother has ever spoiled her child as much as Truus did this thing here . . ."

For a moment it looked as if tears were going to fill Takes's eyes, but it didn't happen. "You know what," he said, suddenly changing the subject, "I saw a film once, about a man whose daughter has been raped and murdered. The culprit is given eighteen years, and the father swears he'll murder him the day he gets out. The man is freed after about eight years: a commuted sentence for good behavior, parole, the lot. The father waits at the gate with a gun in his pocket, and all day long you see them getting along fine and chatting together. He doesn't shoot him in the end, because he understands that the other is just another miserable victim of circumstances."

Upstairs the phone was ringing. As Takes slowly made his way to the door, he finished the story. "Last shot: the father remains standing while you see the other guy running away with his suitcase along a path through the forest. Then you see a white speck appear on his back which moves forward and grows into the letters THE END. And at that moment one thing became very clear to me, namely, that the father, in spite of all his broad-mindedness, should have pulled out his revolver and shot the other in the back. Because his daughter had not been killed on account of circumstances, but by that particular man. And if you don't follow through, then what you're saying is that all those who have lived under unfortunate conditions are potential rapists and murderers. I'll be right back."

The basement was silent, but the violence that Takes had evoked hung there like an inaudible echo. The defective fluorescent tubes went on blinking. With his back to the pistol, Anton sat on the edge of the table and looked at the lips hanging over the North Sea. He would have pressed his

145

mouth to them, but didn't dare. The face on the photograph smiled back at him. Wherever he was, she kept looking at him without moving her eyes. She could look at hundreds of people at once, just as she had when the photograph was taken, and never age, and never see anything herself. And so, with Saskia's eyes, she had looked at him that time in the dark, past him, through him. Wounded, having just killed a murderer, she was on the eve of God knows what torture and her execution in the dunes.

With his hands he covered his face that she had touched, and closed his eyes. The world is hell, he thought, hell. Even if we had heaven on earth tomorrow, it couldn't be perfect because of all that's happened. Never again could things be set right. Life on this planet was a failure, a big flop; better that it should never have begun. Not until it ended, and with it every single memory of all those death throes, would the world return to order.

Suddenly there was a terrible stench. He opened his eyes. A blue pillar of smoke was rising straight from the ashtray. He dumped his leftover whisky on the glowing mess, which only made it worse. In the corner he saw a kitchen faucet over a low, square sink, but when he tried to pick up the ashtray he burned his fingers. He took his glass to the sink. After letting some water run over his fingers, he filled the glass and emptied it into the ashtray. The contents turned into a disgusting black brew, and smoke billowed up to the low ceiling. After he had tried in vain to open the transom window, he left the basement.

In the hall he remembered the gun on the table. Since the key was still in the lock, he turned it and went upstairs.

Takes stood in his room, looking out. The receiver was back on the hook. Outside the sirens sounded, and the roar of the crowd.

"Here's the key," said Anton. "It stinks downstairs. The ashtray caught fire."

Takes turned to him.

"Do you remember that man sitting next to me, yesterday in the café?"

"Of course," said Anton. "It was me."

"The one on the other side, the one I was talking to."

"Vaguely."

"He just committed suicide."

Anton felt he couldn't take much more. "Why?" he whispered, almost inaudibly.

"He kept his word," said Takes, not really talking to Anton anymore. "When Lages's sentence was commuted in 1952, he predicted: 'Now you'll see, they'll let him out too, but if they do, I'll blow my brains out.' And we used to laugh at him, saying he'd live as long as Methuselah . . ."

Anton stared at his back a few minutes longer, then turned and left the room. In the hall the old man wearing the pajama top had disappeared. Behind a door a smoldering voice on the radio sang, "Red roses for a blue lady . . ."

LAST
EPISODE

1 9 8 1

And then . . . and then . . . and then . . . Time passes. "That, at least, is behind us," we say, "but what still lies ahead?" The way we word it, it's as if our backs were turned to the past as we look toward the future; and that is, in fact, how we actually think of it: the future in front, the past behind. To dynamic personalities, the present is a ship that drives its bow through the rough seas of the future. To more passive ones, it is rather like a raft drifting along with the tide. There is, of course, something wrong with both these images, for if time is movement, then it must be moving through another kind of time, and the secondary time through yet another; and thus time is endlessly multiplied. This is the kind of concept that does not please philosophers, but then, inventions of the heart have little to do with those of the intellect.

Besides, whoever keeps the future in front of him and the past at his back is doing something else that is hard to imagine. For the image implies that events somehow already exist in the future, reach the present at a determined moment, and finally come to rest in the past. But nothing exists in the future; it is empty; one might die at any minute. Therefore such a person has his face turned toward the void, whereas it is the past behind him that is visible, stored in the memory.

This is why when the Greeks speak of the future, they say, "What do we still have behind us?" And in this sense Anton Steenwijk was a Greek. He too stood with his back to the future and his face toward the past. Whenever he thought about time, which he did once in a while, he did not conceive of events as coming out of the future to move through the present into the past. Instead, they developed out of the past in the present on their way to an unknown future. This always reminded him of an experiment he once made in his uncle's attic that he described as "artificial life." Into a solution of water glass (the slimy liquid in which his mother had preserved eggs at the beginning of the War) he had dropped a few crumbs of copper sulfate, those crystals of an unforgettable blue which he saw again much later in Padua, in Giotto's frescoes. These began to spread out like worms, billowing out further and further, and there, in his attic room, sprouting ever-lengthening blue branches through the lifeless pallor of the water glass.

He went on a honeymoon to Padua with his second wife, Liesbeth. This was in 1968, a year after his divorce from Saskia. Liesbeth, an art-history student, had a part-time administrative job in the ultramodern hospital where he worked, a place where nothing functioned properly but where he earned more. Her father had married just before the war, and as a young colonial administrator had returned to his post in the Dutch East Indies just in time to get himself put into a Japanese concentration camp. He had even worked on the railroads in Burma—but like Anton, he did not like to talk about his experiences in the War. Liesbeth, who was born shortly after her parents' repatriation, had no connection with all that. Her eyes were blue but her hair was dark-brown, almost black. Although she had never been in Indonesia and there was no Indonesian blood in the family, there was something Eastern about her expression and the way she moved. It made Anton wonder whether there wasn't some truth to Lysenko's claim that even acquired characteristics can become hereditary.

Their son was born a year after they got married, and they called him Peter. Because Saskia and Sandra were still living in his first house, he bought another one with a garden in Amsterdam South. Taking his son in his arms, he sometimes marveled that the child was much further removed from the Second World War than he himself had been from the First. What had the First World War meant to him? Less than the Peloponnesian War. And although he had never thought about it before, he realized that the Second World War meant just as little to his daughter Sandra.

From then on he spent his holidays in Tuscany, in a roomy old house on the outskirts of a village near Sienna. He bought it for very little and had it remodeled by a local contractor. The rear of the house was carved out of the rock cliff behind it, and in one room the surface of the stone was left bare. It broke through the plaster in a crooked, veined, brownish-yellow streak. He loved to touch the rock with his hands; it gave him the feeling that he was in touch with the whole world here in his own room. He drove the family to Tuscany in their big station wagon even at Christmastime, and soon he began to live from vacation to vacation. Sitting on his terrace in the shade of the olive tree, he could look out over the green hills, the vineyards, the cypresses, the oleanders, and here and there a square, crenellated tower in that wondrous landscape which was not only what it appeared at first glance, but looked now like a backdrop for the Renaissance and the next minute like a setting for Roman antiquity, and which in any event was far, far removed from Haarlem during the wartime winter of nineteen forty-five. He was barely forty years old when he began to consider the prospect of retiring here as soon as Peter was grown and out of the house.

One day he realized that he was the owner of four houses. For since he also needed a weekend place, he had bought a small farm in Gelderland chosen for him by De Graaff. Of course Saskia and Sandra were welcome to use it, just as they did the house in Tuscany whenever their holidays permitted. Saskia was remarried, to an oboist somewhat younger than she. He had an international reputation, a temperament that was unfailingly cheerful, and a child of his own. Probably he would collect his own houses in due

153

time. (Mrs. De Graaff hadn't much approved of that marriage, but Saskia had never been like her friends—girls with pleated skirts, flat shoes, silk scarves around their necks, and pearl necklaces, who cared more about their social life than anything else.) A few times the four of them had gone on vacation together with all three children. Often Liesbeth showed some jealousy when it became apparent that Anton and Saskia's relationship was a particularly close one, but Saskia's husband only laughed. He understood very well that it was just because of this intimacy that their marriage had not survived. Liesbeth, the youngest of the four parents, could not grasp these subtleties; yet perhaps as a consequence she was the strongest of them all. At times they called her Mama, which amused Anton.

His migraine headaches seemed to be diminishing as he grew older, but in his forties he developed some other complications. He felt tired and depressed, nightmares troubled his sleep, and the minute he woke up he was plagued by worries and anxieties: about having too many houses, about Sandra, whom he had abandoned, and so on. Like a drifting autumn leaf, a shred of despair rustled about inside him.

It was the kind of despair he had so far experienced only when a patient died under his hands. Suddenly a human being would change into offal. Anton would straighten up, the others in the operating room would draw themselves up in silence, the machines would be turned off. With one hand he would remove the mask from his mouth, with the other he'd pull off his cap and, dragging his feet, his head to one side, he'd walk out of the operating room.

One hot day in Italy, he suddenly found himself in the midst of a crisis which proved to be not just the climax but also the end of those months filled with anxiety. Because the village butcher never had anything but veal, Liesbeth had gone shopping in Sienna with Peter. Anton usually did the marketing in town himself, if only to hang around the café terraces on Il Campo, the incomparable age-old, shell-shaped square which is yet another proof that no progress has been made in architecture. But that morning he had felt unwell and decided to stay at home. He had been reading a little, and suddenly he looked up, disturbed by the silence. His eyes fell on the white table lighter with dice markings, a present from Liesbeth's parents. Restless, he began to wander through the whitewashed, irregularly shaped rooms and went down the spiral staircase with the uneven steps. Now and then he tried to sit down, but this made it so much worse that he stood up at once.

What was getting worse? He didn't hurt anywhere, he had no fever, everything was all right; yet at the same time everything was all wrong. He wanted Liesbeth and Peter. They must come back at once; something was happening to him that he didn't understand. Frantically he walked to the edge of the terrace, but the country road stretched empty into the distance until it disappeared around the mountain with the collapsed mill. He went inside, then out the front door. He climbed the steep steps to the road, which passed at the level of the roof. Perhaps they had returned and gone for a walk; but the car was not in its place. The square, treeless and much too big for the village, looked as if it had been flooded with boiling water. Crossing it were an old man and an old woman, two charred figures in the blinding sun. Meanwhile a few old men sat in the black shadow of the church.

And now, as he stood there, a gray mountain rose up, a tidal wave that broke all about him. He ran downstairs two steps at a time, slammed the door behind him, and looked all around, trembling. The motionless whitewashed walls screamed their whiteness into his face; the curve of the staircase, the rough-hewn beams, everything had become so menacing that something wrenched loose in his head. The rock broke through the plaster and through his brain. Clasping his chest with both hands, he went out on the terrace. The cypresses were flames of black fire everywhere on the hills. His teeth were chattering like those of a small child coming out of the sea, but there was nothing he could do. Something was wrong with the world, not with him. The crickets chirped. Gasping, he entered the house and stepped on the red tiles. Above the fireplace hung his old mirror, the one with the putti. The black eyes of the dice! He knew that he should control himself and breathe regularly, so it wouldn't get the better of him. He sat down at the table on a straight-backed chair, one of those slightly undersized Italian chairs with a rush seat, buried his nose and mouth in his hands, closed his eyes, and tried to calm down.

Liesbeth found him this way, motionless but trembling, like a statue during an earthquake. When she saw the look in his eyes she didn't ask him if she should call a doctor, just called one. Anton looked at Peter and tried to laugh. Then his eyes fell on the full shopping bag Liesbeth had left on the table. On top lay a package. Its paper wrap came undone, unfolded like a flower, and revealed a bloody hunk of meat.

The doctor came at once and assured him that this sort of thing was to be expected, that one should not be surprised by such symptoms. He gave Anton an injection, after which he slept for fifteen hours. The next morning he woke up refreshed. The doctor also left a prescription for Valium to be taken if the symptoms should return, but Anton tore it up at once. He could have written his own prescription, but he knew that if he once began taking tranquilizers, he would never stop.

After this he had a few more spells, but less intense each time. Finally they did not return, as if they had been intimidated by his tearing up the prescription, his making it clear who was master.

The only permanent victim of this incident was his house and the terrace view. From that afternoon they lost something of their perfection, the way a beautiful face is blemished by a scar.

Time passed. His hair turned gray prematurely, but he did not grow bald like his father. As the proletariat was vanishing, the appearance of people all around him grew more proletarian, but he himself continued to wear English tweed jackets and checked shirts with a tie. Gradually he reached the time of life when he met old people whom he had known at the age he was now. This was a strange experience. It made him look differently at both old and young, and himself as well. One day he became older than his father had ever been, and he felt as if he were trespassing and deserved a scolding: *Quod licet Jovi, non licet bovi!* He had always avoided using old saws such as "What's done cannot be undone," or "Let well enough alone," or "When you own the store, you never have any fun." But now he had reached the age where these sayings seemed to express things exactly. He had come to discover that they were not just embarrassing clichés, but summed up the essence, the concentrated experience of entire generations. Usually they were rather discouraging truths, of course, rather than slogans expressing the wisdom of revolutionaries, for revolutionaries are not wise. But he had never been a rebel; it was not to be expected, in view of his experience.

After the death of his aunt, he placed her framed photograph next to his uncle's on his desk at the hospital. De Graaff also died, in the second half of the seventies, and at his cremation there were considerably fewer people than at the funeral ten years earlier, where Anton had met Takes. Henk was there, his mustache now gray, and Jaap, with snow-white locks, but the minister and the mayor had died, and so had the clergyman, the poet, and the editor. Takes, whom Anton had not seen again, was also missing. When

157

he inquired, however, everyone assured him that Takes must still be alive, even though no one had heard of him for years. A few weeks later his former mother-in-law died too. For the second time he stood in the crematorium next to Sandra, Saskia, and her husband and saw the coffin sink into the fiery pit. He was surprised that no one had thought of depositing her shiny black cane with the silver handle on top of the lid, as they would have done if she had been a general.

The War, though periodically revived in books and TV programs, had gradually become a thing of the past, if one can say such a thing. Somewhere behind the horizon, the murder of Ploeg was rusting away until it became a minor incident that almost no one but Anton remembered much about, a frightening fairy tale from long ago.

When Sandra was sixteen, she announced one day that it was time she saw where her grandfather and grandmother and uncle had met their end. Both Saskia and Liesbeth thought this a bad idea, but Anton found it perfectly reasonable, and so one Saturday afternoon in May he took his daughter to Haarlem. They drove along a four-lane highway through endless neighborhoods of apartment buildings where the peat diggings had once been, and over bridges three stories high that had swallowed the canal traffic. He hadn't been back here in a good quarter of a century. He hadn't even shown the place to Saskia and Liesbeth.

This was the spot—and he burst out laughing. The missing tooth had been replaced by a golden one. Where his house had once stood now rose a low white structure in the style of the sixties, with wide windows, a flat roof, and a built-in garage. By the fence around the impeccable lawn was a sign: For Sale.

He noticed that the Beumers's house had been remodeled. Now there was a single large area downstairs, with a new skylight on one side. The Aarts's house, farthest to the right, had a sign in the yard announcing the presence of a notary public. None of the three older houses still carried the boards with their names. He couldn't remember which one had been called Hideaway and which Bide-a-Wee, but he did know that the other neighbors, the Kortewegs, had lived in Home at Last. Cottages had been built on both sides of the four houses, and on the empty lots behind them a new neighborhood had sprung up, streets and all. Across the water where the meadows used to reach clear to Amsterdam, a whole new suburb now lay in the sun, with apartment buildings, offices, and wide, busy avenues. Only a few of the little old houses, and the mill further on, remained at the water's edge.

He described what it used to look like, but he could tell that Sandra had trouble imagining it, just as he was unable to recreate the meaning of that winter of starvation. Standing on the other side of the street with its herringbone pattern, he tried to tell her what Carefree had looked like, to resurrect the ghost of the old house with the thatched roof and the bay windows, when a bare-chested man in blue jeans appeared out of its stylish replacement. Could he be of any help? Anton said he was showing his daughter the place where he used to live, and the man replied that they were welcome to step inside and have a look. His name was Stommel. Sandra gave her father a questioning glance; after all, this wasn't the house where he had lived. But Anton pursed his lips and lowered his eyes, from which she concluded that it was better to leave it at that. He realized that Stommel had interpreted his story as the alibi of a prospective buyer. As they crossed the street, Anton let his gaze wander toward a certain place near the sidewalk, but he was no longer able to locate it precisely.

Inside, everything was bright and airy. In place of the hall, the living room, and the dining room with the table beneath the lamp, a pale-blue carpet now reached from the paneled kitchen-dinette on one side, to the white piano on the other. In a corner two boys lay on their stomachs in front of the

TV and never looked up. As he was showing them the sunny bedrooms in back, Stommel explained that he had bought the house only five years ago. Now, unfortunately, he had to sell because of unforeseen circumstances, but he was willing to take a loss. They walked a few steps in the garden. The hedge through which he had crept so many times no longer existed. The neighbors in what was formerly Home at Last, a tanned elderly gentleman and a white-haired Indonesian lady, were sitting under an umbrella in their yard. It took Anton a while to realize that this was the nice young pair with the two small children. Now Mrs. Stommel appeared, wearing lots of makeup, and introduced herself. Much too eagerly she offered them something to drink, but Anton thanked them for showing the house and took leave. Before shaking hands, Stommel quickly wiped his palms on the sides of his pants, removing only some of the dampness.

He and Sandra walked arm in arm to the monument at the end of the quay. The towpath had been replaced by a wooden partition. The rhododendrons had grown into a massive wall covered with heavy clusters of blossoms, between which the stylized Egyptian statue of a woman had weathered. Unbelieving, Sandra looked at her family name on the bronze inscription. Clearly she would never quite be able to understand what had happened here. Anton, on the other hand, read the name below his mother's: "J. Takes." He remembered Takes saying that his youngest brother had been one of the hostages, but it had never occurred to him that the name would also be recorded here. He nodded, and Sandra asked what was the matter. He said that nothing was.

Somewhat later they sat on the crowded terrace of a restaurant in the Haarlemmer Hout, former site of the Ortskommandantur garage (a new bank building had replaced the Ortskommandantur itself). Realizing that he had never before returned here and never would again, he told Sandra about his conversation with Truus Coster that night in the cellar under the police station in Heemstede. Sandra couldn't understand why he spoke of Truus with such warmth. Hadn't she been the cause of all that had happened? Anton felt a great weariness. He shook his head and said, "Everyone did what he did, and not anything else."

And at that instant he knew for certain that Truus Coster had told him the same thing, word for word, or almost. Then all of a sudden, almost thirty-five years later, he heard her voice, faint and distant: ". . . he thinks that I don't love him . . ." Frozen, he listened, but all grew silent once more; nothing followed. Tears came to his eyes. Everything was still there, not a thing had disappeared—the peace and light between the tall, straight birches, a row of smaller trees where the trench had been. Here he had gotten into the truck with Schulz, while it was raining icicles. He felt Sandra's hand on his arm and covered it with his own, but he was afraid that he might start to cry and didn't face her. Gently Sandra asked whether he had ever visited her grave. When he shook his head, she suggested that they do it now.

Sandra wanted to buy a red rose with her own pocket money, but she came out of the flower shop with one that was purple, almost blue. The red ones were sold out. They drove to the military cemetery in the dunes and parked the car near some others standing in the half-empty parking lot. Then they walked along a winding path toward the flag waving on top of the dune. All they could hear was the buzzing of insects in the bushes, and later the flapping of the flag.

Inside a walled, rectangular area lay the geometrical plots of some hundred graves, all visible at a glance. They were surrounded with immaculately raked gravel. A man was watering with a hose. Here and there old people brought flowers to the graves or sat whispering on the benches. A few people rested in the shade of a high wall on which names were inscribed in bronze. Anton, surprised at not recognizing anyone, realized that he had half-expected to meet Takes himself. Sandra asked the gardener if he knew where Truus Coster's grave was, and he pointed out the plot next to them.

CATHARINA GEERTRUIDA COSTER
16.9.1920
17.11.1945

Sandra laid her blue rose on the gravestone. Side by side they stood looking down at it. In the silence, the flag flapping, the rope hitting the mast, were more mournful than any music. Deep down there, beneath the sand, it was much darker than it had been in the cell, thought Anton. He looked around at the mathematical precision of the plots, all that was left of the chaotic misery of the War. He thought, I should look Takes up, if he's still alive, and tell him that she loved him.

But when he went to the Nieuwe Zijds Voorburgwal on the afternoon of the next day, he found that The Otter had been torn down—apparently some time ago, for the advertising placards were already layers deep on the green-painted scaffolding. Since he couldn't find Takes in the telephone book either, he left it at that.

Not until two years later, on May 5, 1980, did he see Takes by chance on television, on a commemorative program that was almost over when he turned it on. An old man with a white beard and an impressive, ravaged face that Anton recognized only because the name was flashed on for an instant:

Cor Takes
—Resistance Fighter

"Cut out the nonsense," Takes was saying to a man sitting next to him on a sofa. "The whole thing was one big mess. I really don't want to hear any more about it."

On the other hand, Anton often saw a small white panel truck driving through the city, with red lettering that said:

FAKE PLOEG SANITATION INC.

2

And just as the sea finally casts ashore the debris that ships throw overboard—and beachcombers furtively retrieve it before daybreak—so the memory of that night during the War in nineteen forty-five plagued him one last time in his life.

On a Saturday in the second half of November, nineteen eighty-one, he woke up with such an unbearable toothache that something had to be done at once. At nine o'clock he called the dentist who had been treating him for over twenty years, but the office didn't answer. After some hesitation, he called the home number. The dentist told him to take an aspirin, because he wasn't about to do any work that day, he was going to the demonstration.

"A demonstration? Against what?"

"Against nuclear arms."

"But I can't stand the pain."

"How did that happen, all of a sudden?"

"I've been feeling it coming on for a few days."

"Why didn't you call sooner?"

"I was at a conference in Munich."

"Don't your fellow anesthesiologists know how to relieve pain? And by the way, shouldn't you be at that demonstration?"

"Come on! You know I don't go in for that sort of thing."

"Oh, really? But you do have toothaches, don't you! Look here, friend, I'm demonstrating today for the first time in my life. I'm willing to help you out, but only on condition that you join us."

"Anything, as long as you help me."

It was settled that Anton should be at the office at eleven-thirty. Even though the assistant wouldn't be around because he was also demonstrating, the dentist would see what he could do.

And so nothing came of the weekend in Gelderland which he had been looking forward to after Germany. He told Liesbeth to go alone with Peter, but she wouldn't even consider it. As if she were a nurse, she handed him, on a little platter, a tiny, dry, brown twig about a centimeter long, its diminutive chalice with a rounded end lying in the middle of a white coffee filter.

"What's that?"

"A clove. Put it inside your tooth; that's what they used to do in the Indies."

It seemed to her a bit excessive, the way he embraced her almost in tears.

"Come on, Ton, don't overdo it."

"Unfortunately I don't have a hole in my tooth—I don't know what's the matter with it. But I'll eat this."

It was no help at all, however; chewing was out of the question. Watched over by Peter, he paced through the house, his mouth wide with pain, like those yawning faces on the signs that hang outside apothecaries in Amsterdam. He was thinking about the peace demonstration he would have to join. He had read about it and knew it would be the largest in Europe, but it wouldn't have occurred to him either to take part or not to take part. He had simply noted it as if it were a weather report. It was merely a symptom: the year two thousand was approaching and fear of the millennium was in the air, just as it had been a thousand years ago. Everyone knew that atom bombs were produced as deterrents not to be used, but to safeguard the peace. If such paradoxical weapons were abandoned, then the chances of conventional warfare would increase and eventually lead to the use of atom bombs anyway.

Yet at the same time, he too had felt ill at ease when the old man in America had announced that limited nuclear warfare was not out of the question, and that it would take place in Europe, where it would be total. He had been somewhat reassured when the old man in Russia had disagreed, replying that it was indeed out of the question because he would then make sure that America was totally destroyed. But in either case, the implication was that atomic armaments should not be abandoned.

He drank the camomile tea which Liesbeth brewed for him, and sitting on the sofa, tried to pass the time by doing one of those pun-and-anagram crossword puzzles. *Can't the Sun God give you a more precise definition for this heap of ruins?* Six letters. It was as if being unable to bite made him incapable of thinking. He stared at the sentence. Though it looked as if it ought to be easy, he found no solution.

Since the dentist's office was not far from his house, at ten-thirty he decided to go on foot. The weather was cool and overcast. With pain drilling in his jaw he walked through increasingly crowded streets. A helicopter circled in the distance. Further ahead all car and trolley traffic had stopped; apparently the center of the city had been closed off. Even the main arteries were full of people walking in the same direction, many of them with placards held high. There were foreigners, too. He saw a group of warrior types wearing turbans, wide pants, and sword belts, with only the pistols and scimitars missing; displaced Kurds, perhaps, who marched, laughing and singing, with the supple tread of nomads, behind a banner covered with Arabic characters. Whether this proclaimed the jihad, the Holy War, he would never know. Soon the streets were more crowded than they had been since May, 1945. People were streaming from all directions toward the Museumplein. The prospect of having to join this mob later made his tooth ache all the more. God knows what could happen if panic broke out, if agitators should get involved! Anything was possible nowadays in

Amsterdam. Luckily, except for the helicopter in the sky, no police were in sight.

At the dentist's office he rang, but no one answered. Shivering with cold or whatever, he stood waiting in the doorway. The Sun God was Ra, of course; that was obvious. Racket? Raphael? Rattles? Those would be to evoke the God. Ra-pens. Those would be the writing tools of the Sun God, with which he would record his definitions . . . In the distance an endless stream of people was crossing the side street on which he stood. When the dentist finally arrived, limping on his clubfoot, his wife on his arm, he burst out laughing.

"You look very fit."

"Go ahead and laugh, Gerrit Jan," said Anton. "You're a fine healer, you are, blackmailing your patients."

"It's all in the service of humanity, all in the spirit of Hippocrates."

He had dressed for the occasion in feudal hunting costume: a green loden jacket and underneath, green knee breeches and long dark-green socks. This made his huge shoe more visible than ever. As they entered the operating room, the telephone rang.

"I don't believe it," said Van Lennep. "Not another one!"

It was Liesbeth. Peter had said he wanted to go to the demonstration. In that case he'd better ride over on his bicycle and wait for him outside, Anton said.

Van Lennep had thrown his coat over the assistant's desk. "Let's have a look, friend. Which one is it?"

While his wife went once more to the bathroom—because later it would be impossible—he aimed the lamp at Anton's mouth and touched the tooth with his finger. Pain ricocheted through Anton's head. Van Lennep took a slip of gray paper, laid it on the tooth, and told him to close his jaws carefully and gently move them back and forth. He examined the paper once more, then took the drill off the hook.

"Professionally speaking," said Anton, "I would appreciate an injection."

"Are you out of your mind? It's nothing. Open your mouth."

Anton crossed his fingers and kept his eyes on the other's gray hair brushed to one side. Two or three seconds of pain and noise followed, after which Van Lennep said, "Okay. Close your mouth."

The miracle had happened. The pain receded behind the horizon and disappeared as if it had never existed.

"How is it possible?"

Van Lennep shrugged and hung the drill back. "A slight pressure. It had come to the surface. Often happens with age. Just rinse, please; then we'll go."

"Finished already?" asked his wife in surprise when they entered the room.

"Now I suppose he thinks he can forget his promise," said Van Lennep with a sly smile. "But that's where he's wrong."

"Do you realize, Gerrit Jan," said Anton as they stood outside waiting for Peter, "that this is the second time you've expected a political commitment from me? The difference is that this time you're making it too."

"When was the first time, then?"

"It was at that party in Haarlem, when you thought I ought to volunteer to fight in Korea, in the battle of occidental Christianity against the Communist barbarians."

Van Lennep stood staring at him in silence while his wife suppressed her laughter. A few streets further down, a voice was shouting through a loudspeaker.

"Do you know what the trouble with you is, Steenwijk? Your memory's much too good. As far as that goes, you're the one who's the blackmailer. I certainly haven't become a Communist, if that's what you're implying. How could I? You'll never make a dime out of a quarter. But those atomic weapons, they've become the greatest menace to humanity. Each new wave of armament is always a reaction to the opposition, which in turn reacts to that. And so they keep putting the responsibility on each other, and the things keep piling up. And one day they'll use them for sure. It's statistically unavoidable, as inevitable as Adam and Eve's taking a bite of that apple from the tree of knowledge. We're going to have to get rid of those apples."

Anton nodded. He was dumbfounded by this argument. But then, dentists were crazy, a well-known fact in medical circles. But perhaps there was something to it after all. Peter arrived and locked up his bicycle. Seeing him here, with the drone of the helicopter overhead and the roar of the crowd in the distance, a strange, gentle feeling suddenly came over Anton, connecting him somehow to what was happening in the city.

They made hardly any progress along the last stretch of road to the rallying point. Between the Concertgebouw and the Rijksmuseum, under a huge black balloon shaped like a falling missile, stood tens of thousands, hundreds of thousands of people, with placards and banners up to ten meters wide. More people were streaming in from the streets on all sides. Through loudspeakers hanging from the trees and lampposts rumbled a speech that was apparently being given on the rostrum in the distance, but Anton was indifferent to what was being said. What moved him was the presence of all the people here, and he and his son being part of them.

Soon he lost sight of Van Lennep, but it didn't occur to him to give up and go home. A minute later this became impossible in any case. The two of them stood like two stalks in the midst of the human wheat field, with the scythe of the reaper over their heads. Anton's anxiety and panic had totally disappeared. Besides Peter, the people around him—against him, rather—were an elderly lady from the provinces wearing a transparent plastic rain hood over her hairdo, a burly fellow in a brown leather jacket with a fur collar who had a wide mustache and sideburns, and a young woman carrying a sleeping baby in a sling on her breast. That's who was there, and no one else. Among the slogans against nuclear arms, he was struck by a small placard that read

JOB: WE ARE WITH YOU

He pointed it out to Peter and explained who Job was.

The loudspeakers announced that in the last half hour two thousand buses had entered Amsterdam. This meant another hundred thousand people. Cheers, applause. The voice announced that thousands more were streaming in from the station, brought by special trains. All the streets leading to the Museumplein were impassable. Yet, thought Anton, the fact that the human voice could be amplified so much was itself related to the existence of atom bombs. Neither the one nor the other would have been possible forty years ago. Perhaps what was happening in the world was even more terrifying and insoluble than anyone imagined.

He couldn't tell how long he stood there. Peter had spotted a classmate and disappeared some time ago. For an instant Anton remembered the bunkers that had once stood here, the Wehrmachtheim and the German administrative headquarters in the villas all around. Now the square held the American Consulate, the Russian Trade Legation, and the Société Generale. Politicians were being hailed, others jeered at, and finally, step by step, the crowd began to move. Apparently not everyone would fit along the official route, for several different demonstrations began to enter the city from various directions. A curious euphoria pervaded Anton, a state not agitated or anxious, but dreamlike, connecting him with something far, far back that had existed before the War. He was no longer alone, but a part of all these people. In spite of the commotion, a great stillness hung over them. Their presence seemed to have changed everything, not only inside him but also in this backdrop: houses whose windows were hung here and there with white sheets, as in a city that surrenders; gray clouds flying overhead; the black missile balloon blown back and forth, sometimes being snapped by the wind, then straightening itself once more:

THANKS FOR THE FUTURE

At the corner of the square the crowd met another wide stream of demonstrators who were on their way to the central meeting place. They let each other pass, laughing politely and excusing themselves. He was amazed. People were obviously not as ill-mannered as he had thought, or else they had become less so. Or did these marchers just happen to be the ones who were not? He must thank Van Lennep for having brought him here. He began to stand on tiptoe to look around. Suddenly he saw Sandra and called out. They waved and maneuvered toward each other.

"I can't believe my eyes!" Sandra exclaimed. "Good for you, Pa!" She kissed his cheek and took his arm. "What came over you?"

"I suspect I'm the only one here who was forced to demonstrate, but now I'm being completely won over. Hi, Bastiaan!" He shook hands with her boy friend, a handsome young man wearing blue jeans, sneakers, a Palestinian kaffiyeh around his neck, and a gold ring in his left ear. Though Anton did not particularly like him, he was about to become the father of his grandchild. Sandra had been living in a rented room, but a few weeks ago she had moved into the young man's place, a barricaded squatter's house. After Anton had explained why he came, Bastiaan said, "Don't think you're the only one who was forced to be here. The place is stiff with police—Look!"

A group of soldiers who had appeared were greeted with applause. Anton noticed that some people were unable to control their tears at the sight of the uniforms. A daisy chain of boys and girls surrounded them protectively, as if they were a bunch of flowers. Anton couldn't believe his eyes.

"Are you sure those boys were ordered to be here?" His glance crossed that of an older woman who seemed to recognize him—a patient, no doubt. He nodded vaguely at her.

"No, not those! That one, over there." Bastiaan pointed at a man in a windbreaker who was filming the soldiers. "Police."

"Are you sure?"

"We should tear the camera out of his hands!"

"Yes, that's a great idea," said Anton. "That's all they're waiting for, something to spoil everything."

"By accident, of course," said Bastiaan with a crooked smile that irritated Anton intensely.

"Sure, sure, by accident. Please behave yourself as the companion of a pregnant woman. I wouldn't mind becoming a grandfather, if it's not too much to ask."

"Okay," said Sandra in a singsong voice. "Here we go again . . . Bye, Pa, I'll give you a call."

"Bye, Darling. Run along. And be sure you get out of that house before the police break in. So long, Bastiaan!"

It was not really a quarrel, but one more mark of an irritability between them which had become almost inescapable.

Van Lennep had completely disappeared, and so had Peter. Slowly Anton drifted with the stream. On their small balconies older men and women were using both hands to make the victory sign, remembered from the War. Marching bands were accompanying the parade and more music was being played on the sidewalks, yet no one asked for money. All of society had gone a little bit crazy. Exuberant punk characters, their hair dyed yellow and purple, wearing black leotards and shiny black oversized jackets from the flea market, were dancing in the trolley-car stations, tenderly watched by people who had been terrified of them until now. Only in the air did things go on as usual. Planes with banners streaming behind announced that Jesus alone can bring you peace, promised to develop your photographs within the hour at Kalverstraat number so-and-so. On the roof of a parked van sat two enterprising fifteen-year-olds displaying their own attitude toward the peace march:

DROP THE FIRST BOMB ON WASHINGTON

At this sight people cleared their throats politely, somewhat embarrassed. There were also banners with MOSCOW written on them in Russian. In the distance at every side street more columns of humanity were crossing each other, sometimes in two different places. Slowly but surely something incredible was happening. There were several different currents even within the stream where he himself was caught, for different faces kept appearing. Halfway to the Stadhouderskade he was suddenly pushed aside by a file of black, masked figures with rattles, fluorescent skeletons painted on their bodies, who forced their way through the crowd—figures of terror, like medieval victims of the plague. He bumped into someone and excused himself; it was the same woman who had stared at him a while ago. She smiled shyly.

"Tonny?" she asked with some hesitation. "Do you remember me?"

Surprised, he looked at her, a small woman about sixty, her hair almost white, and very light, rather bulging eyes behind thick glasses.

"You'll have to excuse me. I don't quite place . . ."

"Karin. Karin Korteweg, your neighbor from Haarlem."

First, in a flash the tall, blond woman from Home at Last changed into the little old lady at his side. Next came desperation.

"If you don't want to talk to me, just say so," she put in quickly. "I'll go away."

"No, or rather yes . . ." he stammered. "I just have to . . . You took me by surprise."

"I've been watching you for quite a while now, but if you hadn't bumped into me I wouldn't have spoken." She looked up at him apologetically.

Anton tried to control himself. He shuddered a little. That dreadful evening during the War had suddenly surfaced again, the way a dark, chilly shadow will sometimes glide over the beach on a summer day.

"No, it's okay," he said. "Since we happened to meet here . . ."

"I suppose it was meant to be," she said, and pulled a cigarette out of an open pack in her pocketbook. She inhaled the flame he lit in the palm of his hand and watched him shyly. "And during this peace march, yet . . ."

It was meant to be. Somberly he put the lighter back in his pocket, thinking: but the fact that Ploeg should have been lying in front of your house was not meant to be, apparently. Once more the old bitterness welled up, the inexhaustible bitterness. Was he meant to be lying in front of our house, then? He walked at her side, step by step. It sickened him. He could have escaped from her easily, but he realized that the woman by his side was almost more upset than he.

"I recognized you at once just now," Karin said. "You're as tall as your father was, and you're gray-haired, but still you haven't really changed at all."

"So I've been told more than once. I'm not sure it's a good thing."

"I've always known that I'd meet you someday. Do you live in Amsterdam?"

"Yes."

"For the last few years I've been in Eindhoven." He kept silent and she continued, "What's your profession, Tonny?"

173

"I'm an anesthesiologist."

"Really?" she asked in glad surprise, as if she had always hoped he would be.

"Really. And you? Still nursing?"

It seemed to distress her to talk about herself. "Not in years. I lived abroad for a long time and worked with retarded children. I did here too for a few years, but now I'm retired. My health isn't good . . ." Once more with enthusiasm, she asked, "Was that your daughter, the girl you were talking to?"

"Yes," Anton admitted reluctantly. He felt there was no connection between that part of his life and Karin; that in fact, it existed in spite of her.

"She looks like your mother, don't you think? How old is she?"

"Nineteen."

"She's pregnant, isn't she? You can tell by her eyes even more than by her figure. Do you have any other children?"

"Another son by my second wife." He looked about. "He should be here too, somewhere."

"What's his name?"

"Peter," Anton said and looked at Karin. "He's twelve." He noticed her startled expression. To put her at ease he said, "Do you have any children?"

Karin shook her head, staring at the back of a woman who was pushing an old man in a wheelchair.

"I never got married."

"Is your father still alive?" As he asked, Anton realized that the question could have sarcastic overtones.

Again she shook her head. "He's been dead a long time now."

They shuffled along in silence side by side through the stream. The crowd had stopped chanting slogans for a while. Music was still playing all around, but in their immediate area no one said a word. He could tell that though Karin wanted to talk about it, she didn't dare bring it up.

Peter . . . forever seventeen; he would have been fifty-five now. This fact, even more than his own age, made Anton realize how long ago it had all happened. And now here was this young-woman-grown-old walking by his side. Once she had excited him, but her beautiful legs, streamlined like airplane wings, had become angular and weathered with age. Perhaps she had been the last person Peter saw. With the anxious, yet relieved haste of a writer who has reached the last chapter of his book, he said, "Listen, Karin. Let's not beat around the bush. You want to tell me about it and I want to know. What exactly happened that night? Did Peter run into your house?"

She nodded. "I thought he had come to shoot us," she said softly, keeping her eyes on the back of the marcher in front of her. "Because of what we had done . . ." She looked up at him for an instant. "He had a gun in his hands."

"Ploeg's."

"So I was told later. All of a sudden, there he was inside the room. He looked terrible. We just had a little oil lamp, but I could tell that he'd gone wild." She swallowed hurriedly, then continued. "He said we were monsters, he was going to kill us. He was desperate. He didn't know what to do. They were after him and he couldn't leave the house. I told him to put down the gun, that we would hide it somewhere, or else they would take him for the murderer if they came in."

Anton kept up a steady pace, his hands crossed behind his back, pensive, his eyes fixed on the street. He frowned. "Then what did he say?"

Karin shrugged. "I don't think he even heard me. He just stood waving that gun, listening for noises outside. My father told me to shut up."

"Why?"

"I don't know; I never asked him. And he would never talk about that night again. But of course, they had seen Peter run into our house; they would have searched it and found the gun. Then we would have been up against the wall as accomplices. That's how things were then: they never bothered to find out exactly what happened."

"So you mean," said Anton slowly, "that your father found it rather convenient to be held up by someone whom the Germans would suspect of the crime." And as Karin nodded imperceptibly, "He was, in other words, making Peter seem guilty in their eyes."

Karin didn't answer. Step by step they were carried along in the sluggish river of marchers. A group of boys about sixteen years old came out of a side street. All had shaved heads, black leather jackets, black pants, and black boots with metal heels. They forced their way through the crowd and disappeared across the bridge on the other side.

"And then?" asked Anton.

"After a while the entire army appeared on the quay. I can't remember how long that took. I was scared to death. Peter kept that thing pointed at our heads, and suddenly there was a lot of noise and shouting outside. I had no idea what he meant to do, and I don't think he knew himself. I've often wondered why he didn't shoot us; by then he had nothing to lose. Perhaps he finally realized that it wasn't our fault. I mean . . ." she said, looking up at him to see if it was all right to say what she meant, ". . . that we didn't deserve to get the body any more than you or anyone else. I had seen Peter planning to put it in front of our house, and . . ."

"I'm not sure about that," Anton interrupted her. "He may well have meant to take it to the Beumers'. You remember Mr. and Mrs. Beumer; they were old. Perhaps he was afraid your father would beat him up."

Karin sighed and smoothed her hair. She gave Anton a desperate look. He knew she saw that he wanted to hear what had happened next, but that he would never ask. With a sudden toss of the head she turned away, as if help might come from another direction. Finding none, she continued,

"Oh, Tonny . . . There must have been a crack in the black-out of our French windows; they must have seen him there with his gun. Suddenly a bullet crashed through the window. I threw myself down on the floor, but I think he'd been hit already. A second later they kicked in the door and took a few more shots with their rifles, aiming at the ground, as if they were finishing off an animal . . ."

Can't the Sun God give you a more precise definition for this heap of ruins? So this was it. Anton threw back his head and took a deep breath, staring unseeing at a banner that flapped behind an airplane. This peace demonstration now seemed further away than what had happened thirty-six years ago. And yet he had not been present in that room where he used to play board games with Karin, and where Peter had been shot through a crack in the window.

"And then?" he asked.

"I can't remember exactly . . ." He could tell from her voice that she was crying, but he didn't look at her. "I wasn't watching anymore. We were dragged out of the house immediately, as if something worse was going to happen to us. I think we stood for a long time in the cold. I can only remember the glass shattering as they broke your windows. Many more Germans came and walked in and out of the house. Then they took us across the lots, where other cars were waiting. We had to go to the Ortskommandantur, but in the distance I still heard the explosions as they blew up your house . . ."

She was choking. Anton remembered Korteweg crossing a hall at the Ortskommandantur, the glass of warm milk, the sandwich with *Schmaltz* . . . He felt in total disorder, like a room that has been ransacked by thieves, and yet a wave of pleasure came over him at this memory. But it vanished at the thought of Schulz as he had last seen him, turned over near the running board of the truck. Anton squeezed his eyes together tightly, then opened them wide.

"Were you questioned?" he asked.

"I was questioned separately."

"Did you tell them the truth?"

"Yes."

"What did they say when they heard that Peter had nothing to do with it?"

"They just shrugged. They had suspected it, since the gun must have been Ploeg's. But in the meantime they had caught someone else. A girl, if I remember correctly."

"Yes," said Anton. "I've been told the same thing." He took four steps, then said, "Someone your age." Now, he must know everything and then bury it forever, roll a stone over it and never think about it again. "There's one thing I don't understand," he said. "They had seen Peter threatening you with that gun, hadn't they? Didn't they ask why?"

"Of course."

"And what did you tell them?"

"The truth."

He wondered whether he should believe her. On the other hand, she probably hadn't known yet that his parents could no longer talk. He himself, in fact, could have told them, but no one had asked him.

"So you admitted that Ploeg had been lying at your door first?"

"Yes."

"And that you had dragged him to ours?" She nodded. Perhaps she thought that he wanted to rub it in, but that wasn't true. For a while neither of them said a word. They walked along in the demonstration, yet out of it, side by side.

"Weren't you afraid," Anton asked, "that they'd set your house on fire too?"

"I wish they had," said Karin, as if she'd expected the question. "How do you think I felt, after all that? If they had, I would have led quite a different life. At that moment I had only one desire—to be shot by them or by Peter."

Anton could tell that she meant it. His impulse was to touch her, but he didn't.

"What did they say when you told them? Was the Ortskommandant present in person?"

"How should I know? I was questioned by a Kraut in civilian clothes. First . . ."

"Did he have a scar on his face?"

"A scar? I don't think so. Why?"

"Go on."

"First he just muttered, 'What's it to me? Why should I care who did what?' without looking up. Then he put down his pen, crossed his arms, looked at me for a while, and said with admiration, 'Congratulations.'"

Anton was tempted to congratulate her for meriting such a compliment, but he controlled himself.

"Did you tell your father this?"

In a faraway voice Karin continued, "He never knew what I said, or told me what he said. We didn't see each other again till the next morning, when we were allowed to go home. Before I could say a word, he spoke: 'Karin, we'll never talk about this again!'"

"And you agreed."

"He never mentioned it for the rest of his life. Even after we got home and saw that smouldering heap of ashes, and heard from Mrs. Beumer . . . I mean, that your father . . . and your mother too . . ."

The woman pushing the old man in the wheelchair had disappeared, caught in a current streaming off in another direction. Led by a woman with a megaphone, the crowd was shouting more slogans accompanied by applause, but the unamplified voices got lost. Most people walked silently ahead, as if a dearly beloved were being carried away in a coffin further on. Bystanders on the sidewalk watched the passing parade. There was a difference between the marchers and those looking on, a kind of chill that had to do with warfare.

"I went to see the Beumers once, a few years after the War," he said. "She told me you had moved right after the Liberation."

"We emigrated, to New Zealand."

"Really?"

"Yes," said Karin, looking him straight in the eye, "because he was afraid of you."

"Of me?" Anton laughed.

"He said he wanted to start a new life, but I think it's because he didn't want to have to face you. He began to set everything in motion the first day after the Liberation. I'm sure he was afraid you might take revenge—on me too—when you grew up."

"Of all things!" said Anton. "It never even occurred to me."

"But it did to him. Your uncle rang our doorbell a few days after the Liberation, but my father slammed the door in his face when he saw who it was. From that moment on, he was driven. A few weeks later we moved in with an aunt of mine in Rotterdam. Since he had all kinds of connections there from before the War, we managed to leave on a merchant ship within the year. We may have been the first Dutch immigrants in New Zealand." With a strange, cold expression she added, "And there, in forty-eight, he committed suicide."

Though at first Anton was aghast, his horror was soon replaced by a feeling of acceptance and peace, as if he had finally been vindicated. Thirty-three years ago Peter's death had already been avenged. What would Takes have said to that? Three years after he had aimed at Ploeg, there had been still another victim.

"Why?" Anton asked.

"What did you say?"

"Why did he commit suicide? After all, he moved the body in self-defense. Perhaps he did it mainly for you. He just helped fate along a little bit."

180

There must have been an obstruction ahead somewhere, for they had come to a standstill. Karin shook her head.

"You don't think so?" asked Anton.

"No, it never occurred to any of us that they would shoot all the inhabitants. They never had before. We felt our lives were in danger only because Peter pointed the gun at us."

"Then I still don't understand it. He just wanted our house to go up in flames instead of his own: All right, it's not very pretty, but he couldn't know that everything would turn out much worse. I can understand that his conscience might be bothering him . . . but suicide?"

He saw Karin swallow. "Tonny," she said, "there's something I have to tell you . . ." She stood still, then had to keep walking because the procession was moving. "When we heard those shots and he saw Ploeg lying in front of the house, what he said was, 'My God, the lizards!'"

With wide-eyed disbelief Anton looked out over her head. The lizards . . . Was it possible? Could everything be blamed on the lizards? Were they the culprits in the end?

"Do you mean," he said, "that without those lizards, none of this would have happened?"

Deep in thought, Karin picked a hair off his shoulder and dropped it on the pavement, rubbing her thumb and finger together.

"I've never understood what they meant to him. Something about eternity and immortality, some secret he saw in them. I don't know how to put it. He could sit staring at them for hours, as motionless as they were. I believe it had something to do with Mother's death, but don't ask me what. You should have seen how much trouble he took to keep them alive through that winter of hunger. It was almost the only thing he still cared about. Possibly he was more attached to those animals than to me. They had become his only reason for living."

The parade had come to a stop again. The street was completely blocked, because all the separate demonstrations were now trying to join the main one. Anton and Karin stood behind a wide banner which was not held taut, so that it obstructed the view.

"But when all that had happened," she continued, "Peter dead, and your parents too, they seemed to turn back into lizards for him again, just ordinary animals. As soon as we came home from the Ortskommandantur, he trampled them all to death. I heard him stamping up there like a madman. After that he locked the door, and I wasn't allowed into the room. It was weeks before he cleaned up the mess and buried what was left of them in the garden." Karin made a hesitant move. "Maybe that's what he couldn't face, that three people had lost their lives because of his love for a bunch of reptiles, and the thought that you might kill him if you ever got the chance."

"How could I?" Anton said. "I didn't know about all this."

"But I knew. And he knew that I knew. And that's why he had to drag me along with him to the other side of the world, very much against my will. But in the end, he didn't need you to kill him. He was possessed by you."

Anton felt sick. The whole story was worse than the partial one he had known. He looked at Karin's face, the tears still on it. He had to get away from her, never see her again. But there was one more thing he must find out. She was still talking, but hardly to him. "He was a desperately unhappy man. Whenever he wasn't busy with his lizards, he stared at maps. The road to Moermansk, American convoys . . . He was too old to try to escape to England, so that . . ."

"Karin," said Anton. She fell silent and looked at him. "We were sitting at home. You heard those shots. Then when you saw Ploeg lying there, you went outside to move him, right?"

"Yes. My father forced me to. It took him only a second to decide."

"Listen. Each of you was holding one end of him—your father the shoulders, you the feet."

"Did you see that?"

"Never mind. There's something more I have to know: why did you put him in front of our door and not at the Aartses' on the other side?"

"That's what I wanted, that's what I wanted!" cried Karin in sudden agitation, clutching at Anton's arm. "It seemed so obvious to me that he shouldn't land at your door, yours and Peter's, but at the Aartses', where there were only two people, whom we really didn't know. I had already taken a step toward their house, but then Father said, 'No, not there. They're hiding Jews.'"

"Christ!" exclaimed Anton, slapping his forehead.

"Yes, I had no idea, but father did, apparently. A young family with a small child had been hiding there since forty-three. They must have been watching us too, but they never knew what was really going on."

The Aartses, whom nobody could stand because they kept to themselves: they had saved the lives of three Jews, and those Jews, with their presence, had saved their own. In spite of everything, Korteweg had been a good man! So this was why Ploeg's body had landed on the other side, at their own door, so that . . . Anton couldn't take any more.

"Goodbye, Karin," he said. "Please excuse me, I . . . Good luck to you."

Without waiting for an answer, leaving her standing there, he turned away and forged through the crowd, going this way and that, as if to make sure that she could never find him again.

It took a while before he came to his senses, but not too long. He joined a part of the parade that was still moving, or was once more on the move, and let himself be carried along by the crowd. It was as if these hundreds of thousands

of people, these endless streams of human lives, were help-
ing him, crossing bridges and canals in front of him and
behind him, swelling with still more groups emerging from
the side streets. Suddenly he felt a hand on his. It was Peter
smiling up at him. He smiled back, but his eyes were sting-
ing. He leaned over and without a word kissed the warm top
of his head. The boy began to chatter, but Anton hardly
heard him.

Was everyone both guilty and not guilty? Was guilt innocent, and innocence guilty? The three Jews . . . Six million of them had been killed, twelve times as many as there
were people marching here. But by being in danger, those
three people had unknowingly saved themselves and the
lives of two others, and instead of them, his own father and
mother and Peter had died, all because of some lizards . . .

"Peter," he said, but when the boy smiled up at him he
shook his head and laughed, while Peter laughed back. At
the same time he thought: *ravage*, of course, *ravage*. That
would be the Sun God *Ra*'s *vague* definition, giving away
the *U*.

And as they came to the Westerkerk, on their way to the
Dam, a dreadful howl of the mob sounded in the distance
behind them and moved closer. Frightened, everyone
turned around. What was happening? Nothing must happen now! It was unmistakably a howl of fear, which did not
stop but was coming closer and closer. As it reached them,
nothing at all happened, but everyone suddenly began to
scream without reason—even Peter, and even Anton. A
minute later the scream had passed them by and moved
ahead, leaving them laughing in its wake. Around the bend
of the Raadhuisstraat it died down. Peter tried to revive it,
but without success. Then some minutes later the howl approached once more from behind, overtook them again, and
disappeared ahead. Anton realized that it was moving
through the entire city, the first marchers having already
returned to the Museumplein, the last ones not having left

it yet. It circled about, everyone shouting and laughing at once, and yet it was a howl of fear, the primal scream of mankind rising from all of them.

But what does it matter? Everything is forgotten in the end. The shouting dies down, the waves subside, the streets empty, and all is silent once more. A tall, slender man walks hand in hand with his son in a demonstration. He has "lived through the War" as they say, one of the last, perhaps, to remember. He has joined it against his will, this demonstration, and there's an ironical look in his eye, as if he finds the situation amusing. So, his head somewhat to the side, as if he were listening to a distant sound, he lets himself be carried along through the city, back to the place where he began. With a quick gesture he tosses back his straight graying hair, dragging his feet a bit, as if each step raised clouds of ashes, although there are no ashes in sight.

Amsterdam, January–July, 1982

Harry Mulisch is Holland's most important postwar writer.
Born in 1927 in Haarlem to a Jewish mother whose
family died in the concentration camps, and an Austrian father
who was jailed after the war for collaborating with the Nazis,
Mulisch feels a particularly charged connection with the
Second World War, frequently the subject of his work.
He has received Holland's highest awards for his novels,
plays, poems, and essays. *The Assault*, the first of his novels
to appear in America, has been translated and published to
great critical acclaim throughout Europe.